Ward #1

The Snake Pit

9-12-19

To Lucia

A great and talented friend who lends grace and culture to our neighborhood.

Thank you
Alex Hunt
(A. Anderson)

Ward #1

The Snake Pit

Alex Hunt

Heather Publishing UPS Box 481
Marana, Arizona 85658

This is a work of fiction. Names, characters, places, and incidents either are the product of the author's imagination or are used fictitiously. Any resemblance to actual events or persons, living or dead, is entirely coincidental.

This edition was prepared for publication by
Ghost River Images
5350 East Fourth Street
Tucson, Arizona 85711
www.ghostriverimages.com

ISBN 978-1-7333149-1-6

Library of Congress Control Number: 2019912026

Printed in the United States of America
August, 2019

Contents

This book is dedicated to
the nurses and doctors
at Walter Reed Army
General Hospital.

PREFACE

In the early 1960's, not many U.S. soldiers had been wounded in Vietnam and those who had been wounded were sent to military hospitals near their homes. In 1964, the war in Vietnam was starting to heat-up and soldiers with severe wounds were sent to military hospitals that had the expertise to treat them. One of the premier hospitals was Walter Reed Army General Hospital located outside Washington, D.C. This was also the hospital of choice for presidents, former presidents and other officials of the government. Walter Reed Army General Hospital was also known by the nickname "Walter Wonderful," a name given by the doctors who worked there. The hospital had established a modern Research Center, a separate building on its premises, which made arguably more advances in medicine/medical treatments during the Vietnam War than any other medical facility in U.S. and perhaps the world.

Ward #1 was an orthopedic ward located on the first floor in a wing of the hospital across an open square from where the VIP wards were located.

Late 1964 brought more Vietnam casualties to the ward, and although Ward #1 was an officer's ward, the level of care was the same for wards containing enlisted personnel. The war escalated in 1965, and the officers serving were generally volunteers who wanted for various reasons to participate in the conflict; i.e., advancement in their careers and ticket punching, etc.

The enlisted men in most cases (in the regular units) were assigned to a unit and deployed with that unit. However, for whatever reason, they were more open and began quicker to realize that war was a delusion with little or no glory. 1965 was drawing to a close and the number of patients grew.

In Ward #1, there was a section at the far end of the ward which became known as "The Pit", later on "The Snake Pit." In 1965, there were seven officers, captains, lieutenants and warrant officers assigned to the "Pit". Although other officers were assigned to "The Pit" their stay and personalities did not linger; i.e., seriousness of wounds or did not fit the "Pit" norm. The officers mentioned in this story remained together for at least one year or more, resulting in a close comradeship, helping each other when times were tough both physically and mentally. This comradeship was noted by the nurses, doctors and hospital staff to include the hospital commanding officer. If one of the "Pit" members was having a difficult time, usually as a result of a recent surgery, the other members rallied to his discomfort what support they could. As a result, the high degree of morale spread throughout the hospital and into the surrounding community. Members of "The Pit" between operations and when mobile (often in wheelchairs), were asked to be guest speakers at various civic organizations. Reporters and various dignitaries came to visit and wanted to know what they could do to help both the American soldiers serving in Vietnam and the Vietnam people.

This popularity of "The Pit" resulted in almost autonomy for the room which was good, but at times could and would exceed the tolerance of the hospital. However, what happened in "The Pit" amongst its permanent (if that's the word) members, would find its way throughout the hospital and no incident no matter how outrageous and possibly fictional, would ever be denied by its members. Nurses gravitated to "The Pit" and married some of its members.

The negative aspect which arose was the fact that some "Pit" members, especially those who had lost limbs, found "The Pit" and the hospital to be a form of sanctuary, a safety net which created a false sense of reality. It took their wives, families and "Pit" members to convince them that getting back to the outside society or Army units was the real world. This succeeded but tragic incidents did happen.

After I had finished writing this story back in 1984 and left it lying in a drawer until 2018, I read some of Senator Max Cleveland's writing about his time in "The Snake Pit" (1968). I totally agree with him about the trauma and the question you ask yourself "was it worth it (Vietnam) and is the healing worth the pain?"

Although my injuries were not as severe as Senator Cleveland's, they were severe enough to get me free room and board for about 1½ years in "The Snake Pit" (1965-66). There were times when I thought it was not worth it both in the hospital and the 50 some years after I was discharged. Most people didn't understand that after being declared fit for duty and another tour in VN (1968-69), the untreatable pain and trauma that came from the nightmares and the ancillary problems, i.e. falling over for no apparent reason. The easy part is dying; the hard part is to keep living (I read that somewhere and it rings true).

In late 1965, one of our "Pit" roommate's wife brought in a painting of a colorful coiled snake with the word "Pit" below the snake. The picture was hung over the doors leading into the area; hence "The Snake Pit" got its name.

In addition to Senator Cleveland, other dignitaries including Generals Norman Schwarzkopf, Barry McCaffrey, and the Honorable Judge Jack Farley occupied beds in the "Snake Pit."

This fictional story is based on true events; some of the names of the participants have been changed and literary license taken in describing some events.

In closing, I cannot adequately describe the professionalism, dedication, and hard work of the nurses and doctors; the hours they spent ensuring everyone received superior treatment was beyond reproach.

ALEX HUNT

Walter Reed General Hospital Ward
"The Pit"

The instant he walked through the main door of the hospital, the smells and noises came back to him. Walking up to the Registrar and Admittance desk, he looked around the lobby and hallway to see if he could recognize any familiar faces. It was a ridiculous thought, he knew, after all these years; surely the doctors and nurses he had known would have rotated to other hospitals. There probably were some civilian nurses still around since they usually stayed in one place.

He handed his referral and admittance request to the woman behind the desk. She looked as if she were part of the décor; probably had been here since the hospital first opened.

"I see you have spent some time with us before, Major Compton. My, over a year last time. The injuries are still giving you problems." It was more a statement than a question.

He didn't bother answering her, as his thoughts kept straying back to when he had first arrived here on a stretcher, after a thirteen thousand mile flight from Vietnam almost four years ago.

"Please have a seat. It will take a few minutes to confirm a space in the orthopedic ward," he heard the woman behind the desk tell him.

He found an empty lounge chair and sat down. Oblivious to the normal bustle and traffic of people walking past, the remembrance of three years ago kept coming back.

It was ironic that he was back here after all this time. God, it seemed so long ago, yet somehow, it was all coming back like it had been yesterday.

The dry taste in his mouth, the stench from the unwashed bodies, people moaning and bitching because the medics took so long to unload their stretchers from the huge Army buses that had brought them from the airfield.

He felt himself being lifted off the stretcher rack, which had secured his stretcher to the side of the bus. The sedation was beginning to wear off. He kept trying to count the rivets and circular lights in the ceiling of the bus as the medics carried him out through the large double doors in the rear of the bus and into the hospital corridor. The medics placed him on a narrow hospital cart with wheels under it, and departed.

After a few minutes a nurse came by and read the large tag attached to his stretcher, making several notations on the tag. As she turned around he noticed that she was a Second Lieutenant, and appeared agitated. Probably because all the newly arrived patients were upsetting her daily shift routine, he thought.

She turned around abruptly, calling for a medic. A young corpsman in a white jacket and trousers, who was not involved in unloading the busses, responded to her call. The nurse instructed the medic to take him to Ward #1. The medic corrected her, stating that all incoming patients were to be processed immediately upon arrival. The nurse blasted him, telling him that there were too damn many patients coming in, and that the wards could just as well process them as she. The medic mumbled something under his breath and reluctantly started pushing him down the corridor. It seemed like there were miles of corridors. An elevator had brought them down to what appeared to be the basement or first floor.

There were at least a dozen pipes running along the ceiling, with peeling paint hanging off them in various stages of disrepair. He noticed the wall also had paint peeling and falling off. What kind of hospital was this anyway? He had heard that it was the best hospital in the Military system. Walter Reed Army Hospital looked old and tired.

A sudden jar of the cart took his mind off the decrepit condition of the hospital corridor. The cart had banged against a set of swinging doors, which apparently was the entrance to a ward. His ward he hoped. The sedation had worn off completely and his wounds were beginning to bother him.

The ceiling of this new corridor was covered with white acoustical tiles, a lot different from the corridor they had just left. He was wheeled by open doors which revealed rooms with one of two beds in them. The thought of having a semi-private room sounded good to him, especially after the long crowded plane ride, not to mention the bus. His roommate would probably be an evacuee from Vietnam also. They would have a lot in common.

The medic halted the cart outside a door which had a rectangular black sign with white letters on it, indicating that it was the nurse's station. The medic went inside and reappeared with a heavy set black civilian nurse. She had a warm friendly smile on her face, and her name tag on her ample bosom indicated her name was Mrs. Foster. She informed the medic that she would take care of things and signed the form handed her. She told him that she was the night nurse and that this was Ward #1, an orthopedic ward.

She had asked in her soft low voice if he was in pain. When his answer had been negative, she told him that she would need a few facts about him that had not been on the medical report. He had answered all her questions.

Mrs. Foster disappeared into the nurse's station and reappeared after a few minutes, pushing a cart with an array of stainless steel bowls, and was followed by a young enlisted medic. Mrs. Foster told the medic to take him down to The Pit.

The Pit was located at the far end of the hallway. As the cart pushed through the swinging doors leading into The Pit, they entered what appeared to be a large wide rectangular room with about a half dozen beds in it. The lights were off and only the small "call" lights at the head of each bed were on.

Mrs. Foster guided the cart alongside an empty bed. She and the medic unstrapped him and together gently maneuvered him on to the bed. She ordered the medic to take the cart he had been on out into the hallway. The bed was soft and smelled clean and fresh. He felt himself relax and sink into it.

Mrs. Foster was busy drawing green curtains around the bed. The curtains were fastened on a track suspended about a foot from the ceiling and reached almost to the floor. By closing the curtains it completely enclosed his bed, except for the head of the bed which was flush against the wall. The curtains left about a three foot clearance around both sides and the foot of the bed, so that Mrs. Foster could move about freely without hitting the bed or brushing against the curtains. She turned on a small table lamp illuminating the enclosed area.

The medic returned, and together he and Mrs. Foster washed him all over except for the bandaged wounded areas, and put a blue pair of baggy orthopedic pajamas on him, with snaps down the sides which had to be left open due to the bulky bandages.

When the medic departed with the dirty pajamas and water,

Mrs. Foster explained to him that she was giving him a shot of Demerol to make him relax and ease any pain he might have so he could get a good night's sleep. As she took the syringe from the tray she asked if he was hungry, that he could get something to eat before she gave him the shot. The movement off the cart to the bed, plus the washing had caused his wounds to throb. All he wanted was the Demerol and some sleep. He told her he was not hungry, but would like some water.

She filled a glass from the silver thermos pitcher on the nightstand and inserted a curved glass straw into the glass. She held the glass with one hand and propped his head up with the other. The water felt cool and refreshing in his dry mouth. He drank long and slowly. When he had finished, she let him down on the pillow and adjusted the blanket around him.

She slid his open pajama arm to the side and took a piece of cotton soaked in alcohol and rubbed it over his upper arm. Putting the cotton down, she tested the syringe by spraying a minute portion of the liquid out of the needle.

He didn't feel the needle as she stuck it into his arm. As she withdrew it, she rubbed the arm again with the cotton saying that if he needed anything during the night, all he had to do was press the buzzer hanging directly above his head.

Turning off the light, Mrs. Foster disappeared through the curtains. The Demerol seemed to quicken his heartbeat momentarily. He could feel himself drifting off as if he were on a cloud, all pain and anxiety disappearing. He felt safe and peaceful at last. The long journey was over.

PETE'S STORY

Like his fellow officers who had been commissioned in the Infantry, Peter Compton had attended the basic infantry course at Fort Benning, followed by the Airborne and Ranger Courses. But unlike his classmates, he had volunteered for Special Forces (SF). It was common knowledge that SF was not good for one's career, at least that was the guidance Pete and his classmates had received from the Department of the Army (DA) briefing team which had visited them prior to graduation.

The SF in the 60's and even later was not liked by the old establishment, i.e. the Infantry, Armor, and Artillery Generals. They tried their very best to do away with them or accepted them as a short term unit which they hoped would go away. This animosity was especially heightened when President Kennedy in the early 60's went to Ft. Bragg N.C. to review the SF and gave them the authority to wear the Green Beret. Any officer who joined/volunteered for the SF could only hope to attain the rank of Colonel. The good old boys controlled the promotion boards.

Pete had enjoyed the SF training at Ft. Bragg and the comradeship that existed among the SF soldiers. They were a close knit group, not only among the officers, but the officers and enlisted men as well, for so much depended on the team effort. The training of the ten man team, headed by a Captain, of which Pete was the Executive Officer (XO) was rigorous and demanding. The team trained and was deployed as a team whenever a Military Training Team (MTT) came up. During his two years at Ft. Bragg, the team had made two 2-month trips to Africa as part of an emergency recovery effort during the initial space flights; his team was oriented south of the Sahara desert, so in addition to potential capsule recovery, they got a chance to visit and work in some of the countries they had read about in their area study classes.

The Military Training Teams deployed all over the free world at the request of the country's leaders; an expanded A Team (including a Dr. or perhaps additional engineers) also depending on the request. The regular team would train the elite soldiers in hand to hand combat, tactics, parachuting, explosives, etc. The length of time a team was deployed depended on the host country's requirements but usually lasted 90 days or less.

In the early fall of '64, the 5th SF Group, of which Pete's team was now a member, was notified that they would be leaving on a permanent change of station (PCS) to Vietnam. All teams were to be in the country by May of '65. The morale and excitement skyrocketed among the SF members. Up until now, only a few teams had been deployed from Ft. Bragg on a six month rotational basis. The new order meant that everyone in the 5th Group would get some real SF experience, i.e. training indigenous mountain people, forming them into cohesive fighting units to counter the VC insurgency.

His team had been lucky in that they had stayed together,

and were being deployed on site as a team to the area they had studied for almost one year. That was with one exception, Cpt. Dawes, their team leader had been assigned to the S-2 Intelligence section in Nha Trang, the 5th SF Headquarters. Pete, who was due to make Captain in a matter of weeks had been given the team, and a 1st Lt. Singleton had been assigned as the team XO.

Their site location was in the Central Highlands near a small Montagnard Village of An Loc. The location was ideal; there was a river and a small lake nearby and their camp was to be located on a bluff above the river. Their mission was to build a camp and recruit Montagnard mercenaries, the latter of which proved the most interesting.

Pete laid out the camp in the shape of a hexagon, erecting towers with bunkers slightly elevated off the ground so that each bunker could be supported by another bunker. Directly outside the perimeter fence, he laid in an extensive mine field. The camp was progressing better than the recruiting. They had been given a goal of 500 Montagnard (yards) mercenaries, and after almost three months they had only a little over 200. These men had not received any training to date, but had been utilized in the construction of the camp. Luckily since their arrival they had not had any VC incidents.

"The camp is starting to look good," Pete told his team while they were having breakfast. "What we need to concentrate on now is recruiting."

"Iquan, the interpreter, and I talked at length to the village chief yesterday about getting more soldiers. He told us we needed a sacrifice, where we invite all the surrounding small villages and hamlets. Most of the Yards around here are the Koho tribe, with a few Rhade tribes north of us. There is no animosity between the two tribes so we can recruit both tribes without any problem," said Lt. Singleton.

"A sacrifice is going to cost you, Captain," said MSgt Brown, the intelligence specialist. "You can figure at least two water buffalo at between 5 to 7,000 piasters each, not to mention the nampi (rice wine), another 5,000 piasters and also bread." (one dollar = 100 piasters)

"Well, it's probably worth it," said Pete, "I'll take the interpreter and go down and see the village chief this morning. Why don't you come along also, Sgt Willoby, you being the resident doctor (bacsi) and all; I know he likes you."

"Yah, Doc Willoby and Sam here could run for mayor and win hands down," said Lt Singleton, "They really love you medics."

"That's because we are the first ones in the area, and they think my kit bag is full of magic."

They made the arrangements for the sacrifice. The chief had been sitting on the ground outside his thatched long house, with his wife bending over him, combing and picking lice out of his long black hair. He had motioned for them to sit, dismissing his wife at the same time. She wore the traditional black and green rough woven long skirt which was tucked in on one side. This tuck could be let out in the event she became pregnant, making it a practical garment. Since she was married she wore nothing from the waist up. Only eligible young girls covered their breasts. The chief wore only a loincloth made from the same black coarse material. During ceremonies he would wear a black long-sleeved shirt, usually with red stripes covering the chest area.

He informed them he would get all the food, 2 large buffaloes, and the nampi and bread. Pete gave him 20,000 piasters. When he saw the amount he smiled and bowed his head slightly. He informed them it would be a good sacrifice and they would get many soldiers.

None of the team members had attended a sacrifice before,

but had read about them in their area studies back at Ft. Bragg. The idea of attending a real sacrifice created excitement and anticipation among them. Doc Willoby started them all on Tetracycline tablets 2 days prior to prevent them from picking up any strange diseases.

When they arrived in the village the festivities had already begun. The village chief and the head men from the other hamlets were all sitting in a large circle. The remainder of the village was seated on the ground a little distance from the circle. Room was made for the team members within the circle, but they were dispersed among the Yards so that no two Americans sat next to each other. A large jar of rice wine was being passed around and another jar to the others sitting outside the circle. This was followed by a long pipe with a small bowl on it; each individual would sip on the straw of the rice wine and then a drag from the pipe.

"The rice wine is very strong," said Iquan the interpreter, who was squatting directly behind Pete. "Also, the pipe contains opium so I would advise that you do not inhale it. I have already told the others."

"Thanks for the tip, Iquan."

The wine tasted like gasoline. Pete felt his mouth burn as he sucked the liquid through the straw. The pipe tasted sweet and he took Iquan's advice and did not inhale but kept the smoke in his mouth for a few seconds, then let it out.

After the wine and pipe had circled several times and everyone was getting friendly and happy, the village chief gave a signal and a Yard started beating a hollowed out log with a stout stick.

Two buffaloes had been tied to stakes a short distance from the circle; a fiber rope of about four feet long led from a ring in the nose of the buffaloes to stakes driven into the ground.

"They have been feeding the buffaloes rice wine," said

Iquan, "so they will last longer, and thereby make the sacrifice better."

On another signal from the chief two young men with long black spears started poking one of the buffaloes with the point of the spear, drawing small amounts of blood with each thrust. The buffalo stood with his head bent, emanating short snorts each time a spear touched him. There was no dance involved as such, among the two young men, they merely slipped or ran around the buffalo, jabbing it. Then the drum beat increased in intensity, and a grunt of approval was heard around the circle and amongst the others.

One of the young men had changed his spear for a short sword-like weapon. The man with the spear was now sticking the buffalo in the testicles, causing the animal to bellow and move around frantically trying to avoid the spear. The Yards enjoyed this new action. More wine was passed around, and many of the participants were getting very happy. The man with the short sword made a quick slash at the left front knee of the buffalo, severing the leg completely. The buffalo bellowed a guttural sound. A second later he cut the right front leg off at the same place, causing the buffalo to momentarily fall down. By now it was making a sickening sound as it got up on its two front bleeding stumps. In the next instant the hind legs were cut off.

"It's trying to get up on its stumps," said Iquan, "that is a very good sign."

The spear man jabbed his sharp spear point into the testicles again, twisting the spear in his hands. The crowd roared, they loved this last act, which caused the buffalo to roll over on its side. The stumps were matted with blood and dirt. Its nostrils were flared with deep breathing. The eyes were rolled upwards. A woman ran towards the buffalo with a long hooked knife with a large wooden handle. With a quick motion, she slit the still breathing buffalo's stomach open, causing the stomach and intestines to spill on the ground. The crowd roared. This was evidently the signal for the younger children to participate, for a group of them ran forward and started grabbing at the warm entrails, stuffing their mouths with them.

After a few minutes several more women joined in, with sharp knives, and started butchering the buffalo, cutting some of the meat into small pieces and placing them on a large plate made from straw or reeds. The plate was passed among the circle first, with each individual taking a piece and eating it.

Pete looked around the circle at the members of his team. Their faces were all ashen, except for Doc, whose black skin was covered with sweat. They were watching Pete, for the platter had reached him. He took a piece of the dark red meat and started eating. He had endured the wine and the pipe, but he was not sure he could get the meat down, especially after watching the torture of the buffalo. The chief slapped him on the back, indicating that he approved highly of the American participation.

The meat was tough, and each time he chewed down it seemed to shift in his mouth. Another platter of fresh meat was started around the circle.

"Don't chew too much," said Iquan, "try and swallow as large a piece as possible; it will be easier for you."

Pete looked around and gave him a blank stare. The wine was coming again; maybe with the wine he could make it. He took a long sip on the straw and forced the wine and meat down together.

"It would be in bad spirit not to participate," said Iquan, reading Pete's mind.

God, the Army is not paying me enough to go through this, he thought. He looked around at the others. The Yards sitting next to them were patting them on the back. The only one who looked like he was in serious trouble was his XO, Lt. Singleton, who was chewing and trying to get the meat down. He had the look on his face of a person about to lose his cookies. The second tray of meat had reached him. He hesitated taking another piece, looking instead directly at Pete, as if pleading. Pete nodded his head, and reluctantly, Lt. Singleton picked up another piece of the dark red meat.

Pete couldn't bear looking at him any longer. The plate had reached him. He picked a large piece of meat and inconspicuously handed it behind him to Iquan, who quickly took it and ate it.

Luckily the whole village was present, so the meat was now passed among them. Pete took another sip of the wine, which was now starting to affect him. He was feeling better. The ceremony was repeated for the other buffalo. When the meat came around again it was a lot easier to handle. No doubt the rice wine was the influencing factor.

"Here comes the final meal," said Iquan, pointing to two men carrying a wooden rack with six dead monkeys hanging suspended by their heads. The rack was placed in the center of the circle; another Yard started a fire. When the fire had reached the desired stage the rack with the monkeys was placed over it, searing the hair on the monkey's bodies and causing an unpleasant stench. After a few minutes the monkeys bodies started to shrivel up. At this point green leaves were placed on the fire, suppressing the flames but causing the fire to emit a heavy white smoke.

The chief leaned over and said something to Iquan, at the same time slapping Pete on the shoulders.

"The chief said this is his special meal for you and the other Americans."

"Tell him I am overcome, words cannot adequately express my thanks."

Iquan translated Pete's words. The chief in turn told the rest of the Yards sitting in the circle. They all grunted their approval.

"Are we actually going to eat those monkeys," Pete whispered to Iquan?

"Yes sir, this is a delicacy. It is not often I have seen monkeys cooked this way. It is a special honor."

Pete rolled his eyes in disbelief. One of the Yards who was tending the fire took out a long knife and cut off the top portion of the monkey's cranium exposing the grayish brain. He did all six monkeys the same way. Taking the point of his knife he took out a part of the brain and placed it on a small green leaf handing it to one of the other helpers, who in turn took the leaf over to the chief. Next all of the Americans were served a similar portion. The other chiefs also received a leaf with brains on it, but with only six monkeys it was not enough to go around to everyone outside the circle.

The chief gave a signal and all the Yards popped the brains into their mouths and ate them.

"If some of the others would like my portion I will be most happy to give it to them."

"No, that would be a big insult. The chief would lose much face if you do not eat it," said Iquan.

Pete looked around at the others, smiling. Lt. Singleton had a blank stare on his face. No one was looking down at their leaf; all were staring at the monkeys.

Pete pushed the leaf towards his mouth. The brains were lukewarm. He swallowed immediately. Keeping his mouth closed, he made chewing motions with his mouth, imitating the chief and the other Yards. He noticed the rice wine was coming around again. Thank God, he thought.

Pete looked around at the others. As far as he could tell they had all made it, their empty leaves were laying in front of them. Again, none of them looked at him, but continued to stare at the monkeys. Lt. Singleton's face was white as he popped the contents of his leaf into his mouth and grabbed his olive green tee shirt he was wearing under his fatigue shirt and pulled it out from his neck. He bent his head and threw up in his tee shirt. Pete looked at him but it did not seem anyone else paid any attention to Lt. Singleton's discomfort; he wiped his mouth on the inside of the tee shirt and resumed staring straight ahead. Pete figured it was time to thank the chief and leave..

"Will we get to sample more?" asked Pete, making a quick silent prayer.

"No, the remainder of the monkeys will be passed among the others," Iquan said with a smile on his face.

"Tell the chief we have enjoyed the sacrifice and that it has been a great honor for us to attend."

Iquan addressed the chief, but repeated Pete's words loudly so that everyone could hear. Most of the Yards around the circle made complimentary responses to Pete and the others.

The ceremony ended late in the afternoon. The village chief told Pete it had been a good sacrifice and he promised many soldiers.

Pete placed his arm around Lt. Singleton's shoulder and walked with him. Not a word was said, but Pete could not help notice the stench emanating from Lt. Singleton's uniform. Pete and the team members made their way back to the camp. Luckily no one had drunk enough to render them immobile. Pete was not sure what time he lay down on his bunk that evening, but Sgt. Brown woke him at 2:00pm the next afternoon.

"I thought I'd better wake you," Sgt. Brown said apologetically. "The rest of the guys got up a few minutes ago."

Sgt. Brown was holding four pills in his outstretched hand.

"Two are tetracycline and the other two were aspirins (APC). Figured you'd feel like the rest of us."

Pete took the pills and washed them down with water from his canteen. His head was throbbing. He thanked Sgt. Brown for the pills. Not much was said about the sacrifice among the members of the team. The general consensus was that no one would believe them if they described it to the people back in the real world.

"How is Lt. Singleton doing?" Pete asked Sgt. Brown.

Sgt. Brown looked at Pete with a straight face and said, "Captain, the Lieutenant is fine, he even went down to the river and took a bath before he turned in last night. Maybe if the rest of us had done the same we all would have felt better today. I need to go down to the dispensary and help with sick call. We have quite a crowd down there." Pete waived him on.

The next few months were spent improving the camp's defensive posture, and training the Yards. True to his word, the village chief had sent them over 300 men. Most of them had brought their families, so a new village had been carefully laid out a 100 meters from the camp's perimeter, with mutually supporting defensive positions.

They had formed the Yards into five companies of 100 men each. The VC situation in the area was starting to intensify. Two small Lambretta busses had been blown up, seven Montagnard women and children had been killed. The two team medics were conducting classes in first aid for several representatives from each of the surrounding villages. In addition they held sick calls for the dependents as well as the soldiers. A food contractor in Ban Me Thout, the Province capital located about 30 km north of them, delivered food to the camp for the Americans as well as the soldiers and their dependents.

Pete was pleased with the progress they had made. Two companies were out on patrol at all times, accompanied by at least two of the team members. Two significant contacts with the VC had been made. Pete had set up one ambush where he had killed two VC's. They had taken two prisoners who had been interrogated and then sent up to the HQ detachment at Ban Me Thout, where the "B" Detachment was located.

One afternoon as Pete and Lt. Singleton were going over the operational fund records and payroll, Sgt. Wellington the senior engineer came in and announced that their shower was now operational. Up to now they had been bathing in the river with the Montagnards. No one had had a hot shower since they had arrived on site.

Pete and Lt. Singleton accompanied Sgt. Wellington outside to inspect the shower. It consisted of two 55 gallon drums sitting on top of 4x4's with a small shower stall beneath them. An immersion heater had been installed in one of the drums to heat the water.

"It looks great," said Pete, walking into the shower stall inspecting it. "It even has a real shower head."

"All you have to do is pull one rope for warm water and the other for cold," said Sgt. Wellington. The whole team and some Yards had gathered around the shower.

"How about initiating it, Captain? There is plenty of hot water," said Sgt. Wellington. The other team members joined in.

"OK, I'll be glad to," said Pete, going into the living quarters. "I'll just get a towel and some soap."

He got undressed with the exception of his trousers, and walked back out to the shower. Everyone cheered as he walked into the semiprivate shower stall and removed the remainder of his clothing. His head and shoulders were visible over the shower stall, as were his feet and legs from the knees down. He pulled both of the ropes at the same time and the water flowed over his body. Sgt. Wellington was snapping pictures.

"Hey, this feels great. It's just like home," said Pete, releasing the ropes, and started soaping himself up. "It sure is going to be a little more pleasant living around here with creature comforts like this. You guys did a super job on this……"

Pete never finished the sentence.

Explosions erupted throughout the camp. Everyone ran for their designated positions. Pete ran out of the shower and headed for the communications bunker located at the center of the camp. Shells were exploding all around him. When he got to the bunker he saw that it was fully manned. He started for the 57 mm recoilless rifle on top of a bunker adjacent to the Commo bunker. A shell ripped into a 2 ½ ton truck parked by the supply house, setting it on fire. The explosive impact knocked Pete to the ground. He got up and pulled himself up to the 57 RR. The thumps from the camp's 81 mm mortars could be heard as their highly explosive projectiles headed hopefully towards a viable target. He could hear the 30 cal MG and the BAR's spurting out their bullets as he yanked back the breach and inserted a shell. Aiming the weapon towards a small wooded rise about 2000 meters away, where he thought he could see the enemy weapons kicking up dust, he fired and quickly reloaded and continued to fire. After the 6th round his ear drums were ringing from the sharp noise of the RR.

He could see the explosions from his shells. In between rounds he quickly glanced around the camp. Smoke was pouring from the supply house and several of their vehicles. The camp soldiers were firing at the distant knoll with everything they had. The soldier's wives and kids had joined them at the positions and were reloading magazines or breaking open ammo boxes for their husbands. Pete kept firing as fast as he thought the weapon could take it without overheating and blowing up. He was not sure how long he had been bending over the weapon and firing, but all of a sudden he looked up and noticed a crowd of Yards and their families gathered around his position. He was elevated about five feet off the ground so they were looking up at him. He fired off the round in the gun and stood up.

It was quiet. Only the smoke and the crackling of the fire in the supply house broke the silence.

He looked down at the ever increasing number of people gathering around him. There was a muffled laugh and then snickering, suddenly the crowd below him was laughing and pointing at him. The women hid their laughs with cupped hands over their mouths, but pointed at him with their other hand.

What the hell were they laughing at, what was so funny, Pete thought. They had just taken their first shellacking, who could tell all they had lost.

"Hey Captain," it was Sgt. Wellington. "You better slip into these." He was holding a pair of trousers over his head walking towards him.

Pete looked down for the first time and realized he was still completely naked. Dried soap, blood and dirt streaked his body. His feet were cut and bleeding. He grabbed the trousers and put them on and started laughing. The crowd roared as he jumped off the bunker and walked toward the commo bunker, still laughing, and waved at the now dispersing crowd.

"I guess they've never seen a naked American before," he said to Sgt. Wellington who was directly behind him.

"Not the way you looked, anyway," he said, chuckling to himself.

Their losses had been minimal, considering they had taken over 40 rounds of some type of artillery. Lt. Singleton had made an initial damage estimate. They had lost 2 - 2 ½ ton trucks and about half their supply building. Tower #4 had been destroyed as had two bunkers. No dead, but 11 wounded, three seriously. The medics were working on them.

The Intelligence Sgt. reported that it was 106 mm RR that had hit them.

"They are not supposed to have 106's around here. Send in a situation report to the HQ Detachment and request immediate air drop re-supply of ammo. It may not be safe for the aircraft to land at our strip yet. Also get our two companies that are out on the horn and tell them to proceed to that ridge to the west of us. See if they can pick up anything. I'm going down to clean up and get dressed."

"Got you, Captain. I'll have this completed by the time you get back. Oh, by the way, our shower was destroyed."

Pete noticed the smirk on the radio operator's face when he mentioned the shower. He was about to say something trite but changed his mind.

"Good," he answered, "We can't afford that shower, if this afternoon is any indication."

Pete walked over to the quarters. His feet ached with every step he took. He knew the Yards were watching him, so he walked as if nothing was wrong.

"You'd better go down and see the medics, your feet look bad."

"No, I'd better not. How about you going down and get some stuff to clean them up with, they are up to their asses in wounded down there."

"I'll be back in a minute," said Sgt. Wellington, walking out the door.

Pete started thinking about what had happened. It could have been worse, he realized. They had been lucky. He was proud of the way everyone had reacted. They had the makings of a good outfit.

A week after the attack they received information from HQ at Nha Trang that a large VC force was believed to be headquartered about five Km west of their camp. They would receive an air strike on the suspected target the next morning, and Pete was to follow it up with a search of the area.

A Forward Air Controller (FAC) arrived early the next morning in his gray single engine plane with White Phosphorous (WP) rockets for marking targets attached to its wings. Together they planned the strike. The FAC had four flights of three planes each, with mixed ordinance aboard.

The Intel Sgt. requested a strike on the ridge 2000 meters to their west, where the attack had been launched from last week.

He explained to the FAC that they had combed the area, and although they had been unable to locate anything concrete, one of the Yards who knew the ridge well said something was not right about it anymore. The vegetation seemed to be dying over a large portion of it.

The FAC agreed and requested the Intel Sgt. fly with him and help pick out targets.

The arrival of the jet fighters overhead caused a stir in the village and camp. This was the first jets they had seen. There had never been any air support in the area before. Everyone had gathered to watch the strike.

The first bomb explosion brought many ohs and ahs from the villagers. The first two flights had hit the target directed by Nha Trang. The last three planes hit the ridge 2000 meters from the camp. Their first strike proved uneventful. The first plane was making its second run on the ridge and released its bombs. Suddenly the entire ridge seemed to light up. There was a deafening secondary explosion within the ridge. Trees and chunks of ground were hurtled into the air. Smoke was billowing from a huge crater. The second and third planes which had been circling overhead waiting for the smoke to clear, now made their runs at the ridge. They released their bombs at a higher altitude for fear of being engulfed in the still smoking crater. Again there was the initial explosion from the bombs and seconds later there was a repeat performance in the ridge.

"It looks like we hit the jackpot," said Lt. Singleton, standing next to Pete.

"They must have been working years stockpiling that much ammo and supplies. Get two companies assembled and I'll take them out; have one of our medics get ready to go with me, and also Iquan."

As Pete was taking the companies out, the FAC flew low over them giving them the thumb's up sign and wagging his wings. They hit the ridge first. Black smoke kept pouring out of the crater. Small fires were burning all around the crater and small explosions were going off inside of it.

Pete decided to move on to the other target. It was impossible to determine what exactly had been stored there until it stopped burning.

They were walking along a ridge about half way to the other area when MG fire broke out near the point of the column. The company commander deployed his company. Pete moved forward to try to determine what the situation was. The fire intensified. 60 mm mortar shells were exploding all around them.

Pete spotted where the fire was coming from. He told Iquan to bring up the other company. They had to cross a small clearing in order to get in position where they could effectively gain fire superiority. Iquan came back panting with the Company Commander next to him. The other company was now returning fire.

Pete explained that he wanted the BARs and the MGs to follow him across the clearing and hit the VC from the flank. The Co. Cdr grunted that he understood, and disappeared momentarily, returning with about 25 men carrying BARs and 30 caliber MGs.

Pete pointed across the clearing where he wanted them. Two of them started across and the others followed. When they had gone half way across, Pete signaled for Iquan to follow him. They started running across when fire broke out on their left flank. A 60 mm mortar round landed next to Pete exploding, causing him to summersault through the air. He was stunned. He must have lost consciousness momentarily, for the next thing he remembered was getting to his feet and running toward the far side of the clearing. His right arm was not functioning; he had no feeling in his hand and his legs and chest felt numb. Somehow he reached the other side of the clearing. He yelled for Iquan to give the order to fire. The medic reached his side.

"Captain, you are going to have to get out of here. You're bleeding from about six areas as far as I can determine."

"Put a bandage around my hand and take care of the others, don't worry about me."

The section of MG's and BAR's were raking the VC, to include the flank where they had come under fire crossing the clearing.

Pete beckoned for Iquan to bring him the radio.

"Base, this is mobile, over."

"This is base, go ahead," came the reply.

"We are under heavy fire, need some assistance. Fire the 81s at max range using White Phosphorous (WP) on the primary objective as a target. I'll adjust. Over."

"Wait out."

"On the way."

Pete waited for the round to hit. He heard a loud thud as the projectile exploded giving off a white cloud.

"Drop 50."

"Roger"

He knew he was taking a chance, for he was just about out of range for the 81s. He was getting weak, his body was starting to shake, a sure sign he had to act fast.

The round landed among the branches directly over the VC position, scattering it's burning white phosphorous fragments.

"Base, give me all you have, fire for effect at you last registration."

"Roger," came the reply.

In a few seconds the area was exploding with high explosive 81 mm projectiles. Pete dropped to the ground, feeling the ground vibrate under the impacting shells. The VC firing stopped.

"Add five zero every 6th round and keep firing until I lift."

"Roger."

The 81s kept coming.

"OK, lift the firing."

"Roger, standing by for further missions."

The companies moved forward firing their weapons.

"There are many VC and NVC dead, Captain Compton," said Iquan coming up to him. "Now you must go back to camp."

"OK Iquan, I'll go. Base, this is mobile, better get a dust-off. I'm going to need some fast transportation to the hospital."

"This is Base, roger. Is it for an American or Yard, over?"

"It's for me, out."

The medic replaced the bandage around his right hand pulling his shirt sleeve down – tying it off so his hand would not fall off and told him there was not much he could do for the other wounds other than bandage them. He told the medic to stay with the companies, bringing the dead and wounded and any VC and NVC back to camp.

Iquan had rounded up about 15 Yards who had been wounded but were still mobile, and together they started back to camp. It was slow going through the thick undergrowth. Two of the bandages on his legs were ripped off.

Pete felt himself getting weaker. His mind was starting to

play tricks on him. He looked down at himself and saw that his camouflage fatigues had dark blotches all over them, even his chest area was wet with the clammy sticky blood. Some of the wounded Yards had sat down to rest. Pete ordered them on their feet and to keep moving. They had reached the open fields and the walking was easier. His mind kept telling him that he didn't have to go any further, that a chopper could pick him up where he was. The idea sounded good to him; just lie down and go to sleep and the chopper would get him. He reached for his smoke grenade with his left hand. It was gone, as were the two fragmentary grenades he kept fastened to his harness.

The chopper would never land without a smoke. He kept moving his legs, one in front of the other. The legs were stiff, it seemed like he was losing control of them from the knees on down. The gate to the camp loomed in front of him and everything went black. He came to slowly, and Lt. Singleton was bending over him.

"Can you hear me?"

Pete nodded his head.

"The dust-off is on its way, will be here in about ten minutes. Just lie still, you'll be all right. The doc has an IV going, so don't move."

Pete looked around. He was lying on a stretcher in the dispensary. A plastic tube was sticking out of his arm attached to a bottle hanging over him. His legs and chest had been bandaged.

"How many VC did we get?"

"The last body count was 31 bodies and 15 prisoners. The prisoners are wounded. I also called the HQ Detachment to get an Intel team down here. Five of the dead are in khaki uniforms with strange markings. The bodies have just been brought into camp. I have instructed the Co Commanders to bring in all bodies and equipment found. It looks like they are building up in this area."

"Go back tomorrow and look at the crater. I couldn't see anything, the smoke was too thick."

"Right, I'll personally take care of it. I hear the chopper coming in."

Pete felt the stretcher being lifted up. The chopper never shut down, they placed him on the floor. There were two Yards being evacuated with him.

"Anything I can do for you?" It was the crew chief leaning over him. Pete shook his head and closed his eyes. They were airborne. Thirty minutes later they were at the 5th SF hospital.

They had moved him immediately into the operating room, where they cut his uniform and bandages off. He heard a voice telling him they were putting him to sleep for a while.

The first recollection he had of the hospital was opening his eyes and seeing the 5th Group Commander and another officer standing at the foot of his bed talking. He was in a room by himself. The door opened and a tall LTC nurse came in.

"I see you are finally awake," she said with a smile.

The Group Commander and the other officer came around to the side of his bed.

"How are you, son? I understand you stirred up a hornet's nest up there." Pete was groggy and thirsty and asked for water.

Pete told them what had happened, about the crater and the ambush.

"You did an outstanding job, Pete. Nurse, can we be alone, please?"

The nurse excused herself and departed.

"Pete, this is LTC Ambrost from MACSOG, G-2 section. He wants to ask you some questions."

Pete nodded in the direction of the LTC.

"What we are interested in are the khaki clad soldiers. We have a team on the ground looking at the area now. Can you tell me everything you have done in the last two months, and take your time?"

Pete related their training cycle and their patrolling each day. The area where the crater was had been gone over at least twice a week at random for the past three months. It was the Yards that had noticed the change in the foliage in the area. After he had related what he knew, the LTC thanked him.

"Is there anything I can get you?" asked the Group Commander.

"Well sir, I'm about to die of thirst. Could I have a cold beer?"

"You bet. Colonel, get that nurse in here."

A different nurse came in, and the Group Commander asked her to get Pete a beer.

"But sir, it's against the rules to drink beer in the hospital."

"Horseshit, I own this hospital. You go and tell the Chief Nurse I want a beer for this lad immediately. Do you understand?"

The nurse departed without a word.

"Pete, I can't go into details but you and your boys, and of course the AF helped, have discovered something we have feared for a long time. Namely that the North Vietnamese are stockpiling huge arms supplies down here and are moving regular army units into the area. No need to tell you the significance of that. I'll be back to see you tomorrow. Again, if you need anything let me know."

As the Group Commander and the LTC were leaving, the nurse brought in a tray with a glass and a can of beer. The Group CDR winked at Pete and departed.

"This is the first beer I have seen in this hospital since I have been here. It's a good thing you are in a separate room or we would have a rebellion from the other patients."

Pete thanked her and took a sip of the beer. Its coolness felt good in his mouth and throat. He drank the rest down quickly and immediately threw up. The nurse cleaned him up and put a clean pajama top on him.

"You are scheduled to be evacuated back to the States the day after tomorrow. That should make you feel good. If you need anything just press the buzzer." The nurse departed.

The next morning the SF Group Commander came back to visit him.

"Pete, I wanted to be here and tell you myself. The General of the US forces, General Westmoreland, and the US Ambassador to Vietnam, Former General Taylor, will be here in a few minutes. I want you to tell them exactly what you said yesterday."

"Yes sir, no problem, I just don't know if I can shed any more light on it, though."

"You'll do fine; I want them to hear it from you."

The door opened and the Hospital Commander escorted three people into the room. Introductions were made. The Ambassador, a former Army General, looked thin and stooped. Pete couldn't help thinking how old he looked.

The US Forces Commander was tall and ramrod straight as always. The four stars on his fatigues took up most of the collar. The third person was the General's aide, a LTC.

"How are you feeling, are they treating you okay here?"

"Yes sir, Mr. Ambassador, I couldn't ask for better treatment."

"Well, I'm glad to hear that. They tell me you have the million dollar wound, at least that's what they used to call it back in my day. Do they still call wounds that; will get you transferred back to the States?" The Ambassador was addressing this last comment to the General and the Group Commander.

"Sir, I believe they do, but they have changed Stateside to the Land of the big PX," said the Group Commander.

The Ambassador chuckled at the comment.

"I understand you had a little excitement up in your area, Captain Compton. Could you go over your activities which led up to this encounter?"

Pete described the building of the camp, their training of the Yards, and their patrolling missions.

"And up to this time there had been no visible VC activities?" asked the General.

"No sir, we started making small contacts about two months ago."

Pete went on to describe their ambushes and the dead and captured VC's taken.

"The dead VC's, are you sure they were Vietnamese?" asked the Ambassador.

"Positive, sir, they were ethnic Vietnamese. We sent the prisoners up to Ban Me Thout after we had interrogated them. We did get information from them on rice cachets which we brought back to camp."

"How far was the rice cachet from where the secondary explosion occurred the other day?" The General had taken over asking the questions.

"About three kilometers due west."

"Go on about what happened the other day."

Pete explained to them about the foliage dying on the ridge above the camp, and the attack on the camp when the VC had used 106 mm RR.

"Are you sure they were 106's? We don't doubt what you are saying, but as you well know, our Intel people have been telling us that they don't have that large caliber of weapons in that area."

"Not only could we see the dust from the back blast from the camp, but we found the place where they had been set up. Besides the damage they caused and pieces of shrapnel confirmed it. We sent the report in to higher HQ."

"What about the ambush the other day when you got hit?"

Pete explained it was well planned and coordinated, that it appeared to be the type of ambush a Regular US Army unit would have conducted.

"That's what I was afraid you would say," said the Ambassador.

They asked about the size of the crater and if Pete had seen the khaki clad bodies.

He told them about the crater and that he had seen the bodies only from his stretcher when they carried him to the "dust off."

"Do you have any guesses who they are or where they came from?" asked the Ambassador.

"My interpreter informed me some were not Vietnamese, but they appeared to be of Oriental stock, could be either Chinese or Russian advisers, sir."

"I don't have to tell you how sensitive this is, Captain Compton," said the Ambassador, "But keep this to yourself. Our intelligence people also have reported Regular North Vietnamese units in Cambodia and the tri-border area. However this is the first time we have gotten proof that non-Vietnamese are getting involved."

"Is there any proof of who they really are?"

"Our people are checking them out now, but right now your guess is as good as any I have heard," said the General.

"Do you have anything else to add, Captain Compton?" It was the Group Commander asking.

"No sir, only from what I hear most of our camps are getting a lot of pressure lately and so are the Regular US Divisions that are here now. It seems to me we are starting to make the same mistake as the French, namely setting up strong points throughout the country with little actual control. We are reacting rather than initiating, which as far as I'm concerned is not good tactics nor sound logic."

"What would you do if you had the authority?" asked the Ambassador.

"Well, I would go to the source of their supplies, namely North Vietnam, and neutralize that country, either through direct intervention, land forces invasion, or through strategic bombing."

"Captain Compton," it was the Ambassador again, "if our plans go as anticipated our forces will be in North Vietnam around Christmas time."

"Sir, that would be the best Christmas present our troops could get," said Pete.

"I feel the same way, but when you have people 15,000 miles away approving each target and operation, it's not easy to get anything going. You take care now Captain Compton and I hope you have a speedy recovery." The General reached into his pocket and pinned the Purple Heart (PH) and the Silver Star (SS) on Captain Compton's pajamas.

They had all thanked him and shook his hand.

"Not bad company for a shot up SF Captain, eh?" said the Group Commander as the visitors departed.

"No sir, not bad at all," commented Pete.

"Keep what was said here under your hat, especially about that North Vietnamese business." Pete assured him he would.

"You need anything?" Pete told him he was fine.

"How about an ice cold beer?" the Group Commander laughed.

Pete told him that would be great.

"It will be here in a few minutes. I'll stop by and see you before they evacuate you tomorrow."

The Group Commander waved goodbye and departed. Pete's thoughts returned to what the Ambassador had said about going into North Vietnam. Pete felt certain that was the only way the US could win and get the conflict over with fast.

THE PIT

He awakened slowly from his sleep. It was light in the room and he heard people talking and a radio playing. The curtains around his bed were still closed so he was unable to identify the voices and where they were coming from. He found the cord with the buzzer attached to it, and pressed it. In a few minutes a medic came through the curtains.

He asked the medic to open the curtains and crank the head of the bed up so that he could see what was going on. As the curtains were pulled back the voices stopped.

Looking around the large rectangular room he noticed there were seven beds, including his own, all occupied. Not exactly semi-private, he thought.

The room was arranged with two beds perpendicular to each of the two short walls, heads to the wall and foot of the beds to the center of the room. The far long wall had a door leading into the bathroom and also a large swinging double door opening into the corridor. There were windows along the walls where the beds were located. From what he was able to see, the room was located in a wing of the hospital, with this particular room being the last room in the wing.

"Hey, we've been waiting for you to wake up so we could find out who you are." It was the guy occupying the bed immediately to his left that was speaking.

"By the way, my name is John Snyder, Lieutenant type, and I have been here nine months, which gives me longevity around here. This ugly Irishman next to me is Captain Tom Connor. He's been here about seven months."

John introduced everyone in turn going around the room.

There were two chopper pilots, both Warrant Officers, along the left wall; a George White and a Fred Sandusky.

Each one greeted him in turn and he had introduced himself as Captain Pete Compton.

"What happened to you? It looks like Charlie did you a job," said John. "What outfit were you with?"

He told them he had been with the 5th Special Forces Group, on an operation south of Ban Me Thout in the highlands when he had been caught in an ambush.

"Hey, we got another one," John yelled, "We are now in the majority and I don't want to hear any more crap from you non-airborne legs."

John explained that he had been assigned to the 1st SF Group in Okinawa. Like all SF units on Oki, his team had been sent to VN on a six month TDY tour. He had been there four months when he got hit. He had lost his left leg below the knee.

"Tom here was with MACV. He lost his right leg above the knee and his left leg has developed osteomyelitis. That's a bone disease, in case you are not familiar with the term. He may look like he got drunk last night but he really didn't. His eyes are always that blood shot."

John was right; Tom's eyes were red and really did look like he was suffering from too much libation.

"Now, old foul-mouthed Sandusky over there is not only as old as he looks, but he's managed to gross out every female in this hospital. He got shot down in '62, flying an H-21 Banana. Crashed into a rice paddy and got pinned down by Charlie; took four hours to get him out. MACV gave him all kinds of medals, made a hero out of him. Caught a couple of rounds in his upper right arm, got infected, and they had to shorten his arm somewhat. He is still having problems and is in and out of the hospital; comes back here every time some broad threatens him with a paternity suit. Right now he is trying to screw every nurse over the age of fifty. Which reminds me Sandusky, that nurse from OT I saw you with last night has an eleven year old granddaughter."

"You guys are just jealous that's all. It's a known fact that the older ones appreciate it more. Besides she feels sorry for me and pays my bar bill." With that Sandusky gave John the finger and said he was going to walk up to the mess hall.

"George over there is the quiet one in The Pit. He is a good old Alabama boy. Got hit in the foot by small arms fire while flying his copter. They are fixing him up and should be out of here in five or six months. George sees all, screws all, says nothing." With that introduction George got out of bed, got his crutches and hobbled off toward the bathroom. As he passed the bed, he nodded and said, "Nice to meet you Pete, we have a great group here, hope your stay won't be too uncomfortable."

"Over on your right is Captain Sam Childres, another 5th SF Group. Got hit in the legs at Dong Da, a battle which I am sure you have heard plenty."

Cpt. Childres looked familiar. He was sure he had seen him around Ft. Bragg.

"Next to him is Jim Brooks, another chopper pilot. He crashed into some trees while trying to get a better look at Charlie. Lost a few of his fingers on the left hand and got a broken leg."

"Like George said, we have a good group here. We take care of each other; seldom bother the nurses or corpsmen. You might say we are sort of a novelty around here, since there are not many wounded back from VN, especially officers, but I am sure that will change as the war heats up. The entire staff, including the hospital CG lets us get away with a lot more than what is good for us. We get invited out by different civic organizations, hotels give us free weekends with all expenses paid, I mean everything. Now the local football team is trying to work something up for us. So as soon as you get mobile, things will brighten up a little.

Each morning the ward doctor would visit the wards accompanied by the ward nurse and a corpsman. The purpose of this visit was to give new instructions to the nurse on the care of the patients. This instruction usually consisted of taking a patient off medication, changing the bandages or getting him ready for upcoming surgery. These rounds usually took place about 7 AM each morning.

The members of The Pit claimed it was Dr. Berg's means of checking on them to make sure they were all present and had not gone AWOL. There had in fact been instances where one or more members of The Pit had not been present for morning rounds, or walked in in the midst of them. In these instances the Doctor had merely told the nurse to make sure the individual came by his office so he could take a look at him. This sporting attitude on part of the doctor had convinced The Pit members that they would cooperate with him to the best of their ability.

A different form of rounds took place each Tuesday morning. This was called the grand rounds, and consisted of the Chief of Orthopedics, Dr. Grange (COL), and all the doctors and nurses assigned to the orthopedic section. The ward doctors would then go to each patient and explain to the group exactly what was wrong with the individual, and the next procedure he felt should be taken in the recovery process. If the doctor's diagnosis were wrong, he was immediately corrected by the Chief in no uncertain terms, at times to the great embarrassment of the ward doctor.

At Pete's first grand rounds, the doctors and nurses had walked into The Pit and the ward Doctor, Dr. Berg, had started the rounds with Captain Childres. Dr. Berg had gone through his explanation and had merely received a nod from the chief, Dr. Grange. Dr. Grange was about 6'5 tall and looked like he could play guard for the Green Bay Packers. When they got to him, Dr. Berg had introduced him to the Chief and the rest of the group. Dr. Berg had explained what had happened to him and had gone into the corrective surgery he felt should be taken to repair the damage.

Your thigh, shoulder, and chest wound and the others except for your hand will be taken care of without much problem. Your hand is a different story and it will take a while.

"Bone grafting is very painful Cpt. Compton, so remember that when the time comes. You are very lucky to be alive, and also lucky to end up in The Pit. These guys are a unique group which I'm sure you have found out already. The morale here is the best in the hospital, and I want to keep it that way. I've been told some strange things go on in here."

There was snickering among the doctors and the nurses.

"But that's alright," he continued, "as long as you guys keep progressing I don't care what you do." He had turned around and was addressing the entire Pit.

"Nice to have you here, Cpt. Compton, you will be with us for a while." With that they moved on to Lt. Snyder's bed. The rounds had progressed smoothly and Dr. Berg looked pleased when he escorted the group out.

"Did you notice Lt. Perez?" It was John talking to him. He indicated he had. "Well, our friend George over there has been seen spending a lot of time talking to her and buying her drinks at the Officer's Club. And I might also add, departing with her." Lt. Perez was a tall extremely good looking nurse, either from Puerto Rico or of Puerto Rican descent.

"Would you like to tell the troops what transpired on your little sojourns, or shall we leave it to our imaginations?"

"Listen John, forget it. When I leave here you can take

over. In fact, I'll put in a good word; who would want a one legged Yankee kraut with no finesse and no culture, anyway?"

"Charlie didn't get my culture. That is still intact and working fine," John said good-naturedly.

"Yah, our nurse Captain Whealen can attest to that," Sandusky butted in.

"Let's be a little careful what we say about her. Word is that she is in trouble with the Chief Nurse," said John." I got it from some nurses at PT. The Chief Nurse is not happy with Ward I, more specifically with The Pit. She feels that Whealen is not strict enough."

"Well, we all heard what Dr. Grange said during rounds today. So I, Tom Connor, US Army type, will carry on in the best tradition of The Pit."

There was another daily routine about the procedure in The Pit which surprised Pete. Each evening prior to going to sleep, the night nurse would come around and hand out liquid refreshments to the patients in the ward. This usually consisted of milk or juice. However, the members of The Pit received a can of beer and a shot of whiskey if they so desired, and if they were not on some form of medication which would prevent them from consuming alcoholic beverages. To the best of his knowledge, Pete had never seen anyone turn down the offer of the liquid refreshment.

This policy was an open invitation for members of The Pit to supplement the hospital ration. As such, on any given day, if the head nurse had bothered to open the bedside stands, she would have found an ample supply of liquor. When friends, relatives or mere curiosity seekers visited The Pit, there usually was a gift of a bottle of some sort.

A nurse on temporary duty to the Ward had asked Dr. Berg on one of his morning rounds about the liquor policy. His comment had been that they would continue to receive it unless they started advertising it to the rest of the Ward or abusing it.

In addition to the free gifts, the members of The Pit could also avail themselves of the Government liquor store located on the hospital grounds. There was no one with a drinking problem as far as Pete was able to determine. Sandusky would on occasion get inebriated and pass out; but Pete attributed this as much to his immature behavior as to drunkenness.

If a party was to be held, it had to be a unanimous vote by all members. If a person was scheduled for surgery or had recently come out of surgery, parties were never held or contemplated. The holiday season was fast approaching with Thanksgiving just a few days away. There had not been a party for several weeks and for a good reason. The doctors were trying to get as much surgery done prior to the holidays as they could, so that as many patients as possible could go home for a few weeks and enjoy Christmas with their families.

JIM'S STORY

Jim Brooks' entry into the Army had nothing to do with patriotism or wanting to be a soldier. In his second year as an ROTC cadet at the U. of Tennessee he, along with the other ROTC students received an orientation flight in an Army L-19, a two seater single engine plane. Up to this time he had decided to drop ROTC after his second year, which was permissible under the Land Grant College regulations. A student had to take two years of ROTC, the third and fourth years were voluntary.

It was Jim's first ride in an airplane, and although of short duration, the pilot, a young Army Lieutenant, had let him take the stick and he actually flew the plane for about five minutes. It had, however, been enough for him to decide that flying was for him. Later, on the ground, the young Lt. had complimented him on his natural ability to anticipate the plane's movements, and recommended that Jim consider a career as an Army aviator.

Jim stayed in the ROTC program and in the spring of his

last year earned his pilot wings through the school's flying club.

Upon being commissioned as a 2nd Lt. in the Infantry, he only attended the basic course at Ft. Benning, going directly upon graduation from the 11 weeks course to Ft. Wolters, Texas and subsequently to Ft. Rucker, Alabama for helicopter training. He had been a little disappointed at first when he learned he would be flying helicopters instead of fixed wing planes. However, his disappointment was short lived, for he discovered that a helicopter could do many more things than a fixed wing plane. After he had soloed the instructors would let him fly alone more and more as the course progressed. On several occasions he received reprimands for taking chances with his copter. However, these were merely mild rebukes, to let the student know that he was being watched, even when flying alone. Jim enjoyed the flight training and was a distinguished graduate in his class.

With the war heating up in Vietnam, Jim and most of his fellow officers were given a month's leave, along with orders for VN.

During college, he had been dating a girl from his hometown and it was generally assumed by both families that Jim and Emily would get married. Emily was teaching grade school in the same school she had attended as a child and thoroughly enjoyed her work. When he told her about his orders for VN she became extremely upset and a crying scene had ensued.

"I'll only be gone a year; it's not the end of the world."

"Jim, they buried Pat Higgin's brother yesterday," she said with tears streaming down her cheeks. "He was flying helicopters over there. Oh, it was a beautiful funeral, with the Army firing their rifles and all. And a major even gave a speech about what a wonderful young man he had been. Is that what you want, Jim? What good is it? Do you realize we have lost over a thousand Americans over there, and it's only the beginning?"

Emily's voice was filled with bitterness.

"I want you here. We always talked about getting married and raising a family, living here in Memphis." She was clinging to him now, sobbing quietly.

They were sitting on a blanket at her parent's cottage. He had his arm around her, gazing at the water skier doing twists on one ski. Neither one spoke for a while, each of them wrapped up in their own thoughts. He had definitely decided the he would not get married until he came back from Vietnam. Perhaps, he thought, Emily sensed this and that was part of the reason for her outburst and depression. In the three years they had gone together in college they had never gone to bed. There had been the usual heavy petting but they had both tacitly agreed they would wait until they were married. Emily got up without saying a word and walked into the cabin. He sat there watching the water skier. After a while he got up, pulling up a long blade of grass. He was chewing on the stem as he walked into the cottage. Coming out of the bright sunlight, it took his eyes a few seconds to adjust to the darkened interior. Emily was not in the front room. He walked slowly into the back room which served as the bedroom. Emily was in the bed with the covers drawn up under her chin.

"I'm naked, Jim; I want you here beside me."

He walked back into the front room and bolted the door. Returning to the back room he sat down on the bed next to her and removed his swimming suit. She lifted up the covers and he moved in close beside her.

"Emily, are you sure?"

"I'm not waiting any longer; I'm more sure about this than about anything in my life."

She pulled him close to her, encircling his body with her arms. On the lake the water skier was making lazy turns behind the boat.

He had thought about Emily his first two months in Vietnam. He received a letter from her just about every other day. His assignment had been to a newly formed aviation unit as a gunship pilot. During his first month in the country he had received extensive training in target acquisition and the latest tactics. His gunship consisted of a HUIB helicopter with MG mounted on each side, which he or the co-pilot controlled by means of a specially adapted sighting device, mounted on their console. In addition, there was also a door gunner with an M-60 Mg hanging from the door. Most of their missions consisted of supporting Vietnamese forces or Special Forces (SF) operations, or coming to some SF camp aid that was under attack. This type of mission was becoming more numerous of late. Although some of his friends had been shot down, Jim flew with complete abandon. It was no use worrying about something that might happen. His reasoning was unfortunately not shared by his copilots.

"I need two ships to fly a recon mission. The SF are inserting some "D" teams tonight and we need some Intel about the border area where they are going in," the Company Commander said.

The other pilots in the briefing room looked at each other. No one raised their hand.

"Come on, do I have to pick you guys?"

Jim didn't care for his CO and the feeling was mutual. Jim had flown more missions than anyone in the company. Yet when a mission came along where they would transport a VIP and remain overnight in Saigon or the resort town of Vung Tau, the CO always took those missions himself. He had never participated in an assault. Jim had mentioned it to him, that it would be nice if some of the VIP missions were spread around. The CO had informed him sarcastically that when he became a company commander, he could run his company as he saw fit; until then for him to do what he was told.

Jim raised his hand. He enjoyed working with the SF. They were the only ones who were really doing something worthwhile over there. The CO got one more volunteer who was to be John's co-pilot. He picked two other pilots for the second ship.

He was preflighting his ship, paying special attention to the MGs and their feeding system. There had been some problem with jamming lately. His crew chief announced the ship was fueled and ready.

They had received their detailed briefing on the area to be reconnoitered; an SF Intelligence officer who was to fly in the second ship. He headed the chopper for the Cambodian border area. They had flown back and forth over the area several times at 1500 feet, when the Intel officer requested Jim go down and take a closer look. He put his chopper in a descending left turn, and was at treetop level in a matter of seconds. He had been flying for about two minutes when the co-pilot pointed down below them.

"I see activity down there, black pajamas and all."

The other chopper was monitoring their transmission. "See if you can determine the size of the force," came the guidance from the Intel officer.

"Jim, swing the chopper into a tight turn." Flying at tree top level he could see VC running for cover.

"It looks like a company size force," he said over the radio.

"Okay, thanks, let's get out of here," came the reply.

As he was making a climbing turn to the right, the chopper shook violently and windshield particles spewed throughout the chopper.

"It looks like we took one," he said to the copilot.

There was no answer. He glanced over and saw the copilot staring straight ahead, his chest covered with blood. The shoulder harness kept him from falling forward. He looked around for the crew chief. All he could see was his back, he was prone on the floor. His back looked like it was torn up with an ice pick.

He tried to gain altitude but the chopper was not responding. "I'm losing altitude and have marginal controls left; also have two dead aboard."

"Roger, we see you; try to keep it airborne as long as possible at your present heading. Help is on the way."

The wind rushing in the right hand windshield area was having an adverse effect on the chopper. He was skimming the tree tops, altitude less than 100 feet, speed 60 knots and slowing. He saw a clearing up ahead. He had to make it, it was his only chance. He pushed forward on the cyclic stick pulling up on the collective control at the same time. There was no response; he was barely flying. He slammed into the top of the trees at the beginning of the clearing. The chopper went over in a right hand bank turn. The ground was coming up fast. He must have lost consciousness momentarily. He tried to release his safety straps with his right hand but his fingers wouldn't work. Looking down at his hand he almost got sick. Where his fingers had been looked mangled he had a thumb and index finger and one next to the little finger but they wouldn't work. He pressed the release on his straps with his left hand and yanked the door open. The chopper was laying on its right side. He struggled to get out of his seat. His right leg would not function. Jim heaved himself toward the door. He managed to get the upper part of his body out. His right leg was stuck; there was no pain in his leg, it was numb. He looked back and saw for the first time that the chopper was on fire.

He pulled himself up to try and see what was pinning his right foot. He noticed that his foot was twisted around the collective control stick at a grotesque angle. With his left foot he managed to kick at his right foot, freeing it from the collective stick. The heat from the burning chopper was becoming unbearable. He realized he had only seconds left. The rounds from the right MG were cooking off, exploding with whizzing sounds. He remembered the fire extinguisher behind his seat. He yanked it free and depressed the handle, spraying himself with the white gas-like substance. It felt good momentarily. Again he pulled with his left hand, at the same time pushing with his left foot. His right leg was free. He managed to inch his way out the door. He fell to the ground, hitting the left skid of the chopper which was sticking up in the air. After laying on the ground for a few seconds, he tried to determine which way to crawl as the chopper was being engulfed in flames.

He started crawling on his left side, dragging his right leg. There was no feeling in his leg below the knee; his foot was flopping along on the ground. He had crawled about 30 feet from the chopper when there was a loud explosion. A thick black cloud of smoke billowed up into the air. Exploding MG rounds were whizzing through the air above him. Suddenly he felt hands grabbing him by the shoulders. Another pair of hands grabbed his legs. He screamed in pain.

"Sorry pal, we have to get out of here fast. There are unfriendlies heading this way." It was the SF Intel officer speaking.

They laid him on the floor of the chopper and were airborne immediately.

"Sorry we didn't get down faster but were busy trying to discourage a platoon of VC from heading this way. Are you in pain?"

Jim had no feeling in his right hand. It was numb with just a dull throbbing sensation. He told them his leg hurt. The Intel officer gave him a shot of morphine and put a tourniquet on his right arm.

"That should hold you for a while. We'll be at the 3rd Field Hospital in Saigon soon."

The shot had a numbing effect and he closed his eyes and dozed off. He vaguely remembered being lifted onto a stretcher and placed in an Army ambulance. The ride to the hospital was very short. A nurse in a white uniform had directed the medics where to take him. They had cut away his uniform and transferred him to a cloth table. He heard voices but could not follow their conversation. His next recollection was waking up in a large ward. His right hand was wrapped in a huge bandage and suspended from a metal stand, elevating the arm in the air. His right leg had a cast on it from his toes all the way up to his thigh. An IV was in his left arm hooked to a bottle of clear liquid, suspended from a metallic stand.

"How are you feeling?" It was a Lieutenant Nurse in a white uniform standing at the foot of his bed." You have been asleep a long time; I was starting to get a little worried about you."

"What happened to me?"

"You broke your leg about six inches below your knee." It was a doctor speaking. He had walked over from another patient." You also lost some fingers in your left hand. The fact is, though, you are a very lucky young man to even be alive, from what I hear. We'll keep you here a few days and then evacuate you to a hospital back in the States, where they have a hand clinic. They'll fix you up."

Turning to the nurse, he asked if she could get in touch with his unit.

"We already have, Jim, someone will be here this afternoon."

He thanked her and closed his eyes. What a hell of a way to end up, he thought; probably would not be able to fly again. He thought of Emily. What would she think of him, having only a partial hand? He felt tears welling up in his eyes; what a lousy deal.

The company Commander and 1st Sergeant arrived the next afternoon. The commander had brought with him a form which he filled out by asking Jim a lot of questions concerning what had happened. He went over the entire ordeal leaving nothing out.

"Are you sure the chopper was hit by ground fire?" It was the third time the Commander had asked the question.

"I told you before, yes. The entire right windshield blew out. The copilot and crew chief were killed immediately. I had minimum control of the ship from then on."

"Well, you see, it sounded like you might have had mechanical failure. We went out to recover the remains this morning and there is nothing left except the engine. There is nothing left of the other two."

Jim was getting mad. He felt himself losing control. "What the hell are you talking about? The other chopper saw what happened. There were VC below us. They fired and hit us. What the hell are you trying to pull anyway?" He was furious.

"It makes a great difference if you were hit by enemy fire or had mechanical problems."

"You mean, you might have to write up a citation if it was enemy fire, don't you? You get the fuck out of here, you bastard. You put down anything you want."

The entire ward could hear his shouting. A nurse came over and asked the Company Commander and the 1st Sergeant to leave.

"You shouldn't get so upset. Would you like something for pain?" she asked in a soft quiet voice.

"Yes, please," he said, laying his head back on his pillow.

The next day he talked to the doctor and asked if there was any way he could get in touch with the SF Captain that had flown in the second helicopter. He provided the unit and name of the Captain; the doctor informed him that he would personally see to it. That afternoon they moved him down to the admin section where there was a phone call for him. It was the SF Captain. Jim explained what was going on and the visit by the CO. The Captain asked for Jim's full name, unit, and serial number. He informed Jim that he had already talked to his doctor and that they were sending him to Walter Reed Hospital.

The Captain assured him that he would file a complete report on what had happened since he and the pilots of the 2nd chopper had been eyewitnesses to the incident. Jim thanked him and hung the phone up. He felt better.

They had kept him there three days, and then evacuated him to the States.

THE PIT

One morning Jim made it in just in time for rounds.

"Hey, you having a good time, my boy?" It was Sandusky.

"You guys don't know what you're talking about," Jim said, taking off his shirt. He had been dating one of the physical therapists, a cute Lieutenant named Linda. It appeared to be getting kind of serious. He, of course, was adamant in his denials regarding his involvement.

"Look at this shirt," Jim said, holding it up so everyone could see it. "I slept in it all night on the floor of Linda's apartment, and not a wrinkle. It must be this new material, nylon or Dacron or something that keeps it from wrinkling."

"Listen, Jim, we all know where you slept last night. No one in this room can criticize you. We're all basically doing the same thing. Except for me that is. I'm married, and with Pat here I wouldn't dare," Tom said.

"Yah, me neither," chimed in Sandusky.

"Well, I just don't want the word to get out, and people get the wrong idea. She is really a nice girl and has had a rough time. I don't know if you guys know, but she was married once before to a real shithead who gave her all kinds of grief. We haven't set a date, but probably next spring or summer we'll get married."

Jim had gone through extensive surgery on his hand and they were still working on it. The thumb and index finger were now basically healed; the fourth finger had been moved to where the little finger had been. The next operation they would do tendon grafts so that he would have a grip and the use of an almost normal hand. He had a cast on his right leg.

The doctor walked in for his morning rounds.

Jim had met Linda during one of his daily physical therapy sessions. They had a lot in common so they started dating. Linda made it a practice to stop by the ward each day before leaving work to talk to him, so it was not exactly a secret. He had refused other offers from the guys to fix him up with girls, so everyone took it for granted they were a twosome.

It had started getting serious one Saturday morning when Linda had come over to pick him up. He had taken his kit with him so no one expected him back until Monday morning.

"You know, Linda, there is something I should tell you before we start assuming too much about each other," Jim said as they were driving out of the hospital gates. "I was sort of engaged to a girl back in Memphis before all this happened to me. She has been up here visiting me and will probably be back unless I discourage her."

"Listen, I'm not taking anything for granted and neither should you. I have no intentions of getting serious and I hope you feel the same way." And so she had told him about her previous marriage.

He sat there quietly listening, not saying a word. When she had finished he had put his hand on her shoulder." I think I love you Linda," he said slowly and quietly.

Neither one spoke until they had reached her apartment door. She had opened it, letting him go in first.

Inside the living room, he turned and took her in his arms and kissed her.

"Oh, I love you too," she whispered in his ear. They kissed again, this time longer and more demanding.

"Oh my God," she moaned against his neck, "it's been so long."

They started moving towards the bedroom still holding each other and kissing. She quickly removed her clothes, helping him get out of his. They laid down side by side kissing and caressing.

"I don't know if I can make it with this cast on."

"Don't worry, I'll help," she said mockingly. "Don't you know physical therapists can make anything happen?" She gently and patiently caressed and manipulated him until he had achieved the desired stage.

It had been an awkward first time, he thought, as he lay alongside her with her head cradled in his arm.

"God, you're beautiful Linda," he reached over and caressed her left breast. She made a muffled sound, keeping her eyes closed.

"My breasts are too large; I wish they were a little smaller."

"You're crazy," biting gently on the new erect nipples, and gently kissing her slowly all over her body.

"Hmmm, I like that," she whispered, gently pushing his head back down again. After a few moments she pulled him back up.

"Now me you."

They had stayed in bed most of the morning. He decided he would tell Emily not to visit him anymore.

Peter Compton underwent over 15 operations before being declared eligible to walk around. Eight split thickness skin grafts taken from his upper legs/thighs were placed over different wounds to protect them from infection until full thickness skin grafts could be grown on to the prepared area. One procedure was done by cutting a 6 in x 6 in x 6 in flap in his stomach lifting it up and placing a split thickness skin graft under the flap and one on the donor site. The flap hung on the stomach until the surgeons were sure it had established its own blood supply. Once the blood supply was confirmed, usually about 3-4 weeks, the hand was then attached to the flap pulled over the top of the hand and would so remain for about 6 weeks and then cut if off from the stomach. Tendons would later be taken from the top of the feet and lower legs and reattached to tendon stubs in the hand and arm, giving him a flexible hand again. This in itself would not be a very painful operation. However, where they took the split thickness graft from, and when the follow up procedures were not done correctly, it could definitely get your attention. A piece of gauze was placed over the graft donor area to soak up the blood, but the blood could not be allowed to harden or congeal for then it became a 4 inch by 8 inch scab that had to be pulled off which felt like peeling skin off your thigh leaving a bloody 4 x 8 inch area. This luckily would not happen often - usually on weekends when a new intern had the watch and was afraid to take the gauze off. So on Monday morning rounds the regular doctor would perform this excruciating procedure with the appropriate apologies.

Pete was starting to settle down to a daily routine. He could walk now and tried to get as much exercise as possible. His legs were still stiff but were beginning to feel better.

It was Jim who got the news first. Wheeling himself into The Pit, he closed the doors behind him.

"Hey listen guys, we may have a problem. I was outside the nurses' station when Colonel Hayden, the Chief Nurse, walked into the station with a new nurse, a Lieutenant, I think. I heard her briefing the corpsmen that this new nurse; I couldn't get her name, was now in charge of Ward #1. That all the hanky panky going on in The Pit was coming to a halt."

"What does she look like?" John interrupted.

"Well, I didn't get a good look, but she seemed pretty nice. She wears glasses."

"Oh shit, that's what I call an astute observation, she wears glasses. That's not what we're talking about, dipshit," Sandusky yelled at him. "What kind of body, big tits, small tits, ass, legs?" I supposed I owe it to you guys to check her out myself." Sandusky got his robe on and walked out into the hall.

"What I started to say before I was interrupted by Mr. Suave, was that Col. Hayden is not only putting out the word to crack down, she is instituting a curfew, especially for The Pit. She still has it in for us. She has never forgiven Sandusky for throwing up all over her dress that night at the Club."

"Well, you and John should have gotten him out of there that night when I first told you," Childres commented; "he was out of it before the party even started."

"Hey, that's water under the bridge, Childres. What we need to do is come up with a plan." Tom had now joined the conversation. "We need to win over and convince the new Lt. that we are really a model bunch of Patients."

"We got company." It was Sandusky returning from his recon. "Col Hayden and Lt Bjorkvik, that's her name, by the way, are heading down here."

Colonel Hayden walked in and asked to have everyone's attention. "I want to introduce you to your new nurse, Lt. Bjorkvik. She is taking over from Captain Whealen, who has moved up to Obstetrics."

Col Hayden made the introductions, introducing everyone in The Pit to the new nurse.

"I have instructed Lt Bjorkvik to be firm and not to be taken in by you people like the other nurses were. From now on you will observe the hospital rules like everyone else. Visitors will not be allowed in here after 2100 hours, and 2300 hours is curfew for everyone unless you have an authorized overnight from your doctor. In that case you will let your nurse know your whereabouts and sign out, leaving a telephone number where you can be reached. Does anyone have any questions? Just remember this is a hospital and not a fraternity house."

There were no questions. With that, Col Hayden and Lt Bjorkvik left.

"Bjorkvik is not a bad looking girl. I believe if we play our cards right and train her properly, she can be fun," said John. "Tom, what do you think we should do, we need to start her off right?"

"Well, it's almost medication time. That means she will be here in about five minutes. I'm sure she doesn't remember all of our names or can place the names with our faces. So why don't we all switch beds? Here Pete, you and I switch, everyone move over two beds. Since she doesn't know us, she will be using our name tags at the end of the beds to go by."

Everyone had switched, and none too soon. Lt. Bjorkvik appeared with a cart full of medications. She was a good looking girl, with blond hair hanging almost to her shoulders. Her face was well proportioned with high cheek bones and deep blue eyes. She looked to be about 5'6" tall. Her white uniform revealed just enough of her contours to let you know she had all the equipment.

"Okay, guys, I have heard all about you and my responsibility as I see it is to enforce the hospital rules. Col Hayden has assured me that she will back me one hundred per cent on any actions I take. I'm telling you all this so if you come down on report, you are forewarned. I understand that most of you are getting fed in the ward. As of tomorrow morning, if you are mobile, and that means crutches also, you will take your meals in the mess hall upstairs. The ward corpsmen are spending entirely too much time handing out and picking up food trays, when they should be doing something constructive. Also, this room will be cleaned by 0800 hours each day and that means you make your beds and straighten out your areas. Now, do I have any questions?"

No one said a word.

"All right then, we understand each other," she said in a crisp firm voice. She started handing out the medications, reading each name tag at the foot of the beds out loud as she went along.

"I'll be back to give you your Streptomycin shot, Captain Childres, as soon as I pass out the rest of the medications."

Sandusky, who was sitting on Childres' bed, smiled at her and said, "Yes ma'am, I'll be here."

As she handed out the last paper cup of pills to John, who was now sitting on George's bed, Tom held up his cup and said, "Hey, these are not my pills, it says WO George White on this slip. I'm not WO George White."

"This is not mine either," said Cpt Childres, as he held up his cup. "I'm not going to take this, it could be harmful. I might even die. Imagine surviving VN only to be done in by one of our own nurses."

"Are you sure you're a real nurse?"

"I want this foolishness to stop, do you hear me? I want it stopped this minute." Lt Bjorkvik was starting to lose control. She was going from bed to bed checking the prescription to see if it corresponded to the name on the bed.

"Hey, will the real Lt Snyder please stand up, because I'm

not Lt Snyder, am I? I wasn't Lt Snyder when I woke up this morning. Someone please give me my medication. I need help; you guys know how I get when I don't have my medicine." It was Jim's turn.

It kept up like this for another five minutes.

Lt Bjorkvik tried again to get order. She was now shouting at everyone to be quiet, but no one paid any attention to her. A look of sheer terror was now on Lt Bjorkvik's face.

"Hey look," said Sandusky, "Didn't they teach you anything, how to give out even medications? Can't you read? You dumb broads put on your virgin white uniforms and think you are a bunch of Florence Nightingales. You'd better shape up or Col Hayden will have you back emptying bed pans."

Sandusky's remarks turned out to be the proverbial straw. Tears were welling up in her eyes and streaming down her cheeks. She sat down on the chair next to Tom's bed, staring straight ahead. Bjorkvik started sobbing quietly. John glanced around the room. No one spoke.

She got up and walked out of the room, wiping her eyes with a hanky.

Tom made the motion with his finger for everyone to be quiet; about a minute went by.

The doors opened and in walked Bjorkvik, somewhat composed now.

"Guys," she hesitated, "Look, give me a break." There were still tears in her eyes. She had trouble going on. "You win, you cooperate with me and I'll do the same. I didn't mean to come on so strong, I apologize. I realize you guys have been through a lot, and some of you have a long time to go here. "Please." It was a plea.

"Okay, let's get our medicine." It was George, as he moved off the bed and back where he belonged. Everyone else followed.

The atmosphere was a little uncomfortable. When everyone had received their medicine, Sandusky spoke up.

"Hey Lt. I didn't mean what I said. I'm sorry. You are going to find out that this is the best bunch of guys in the hospital."

She looked around at everyone, smiling shyly.

"Col Hayden has it in for me and the whole Pit. It seems I ruined her dress one night at the O club. We haven't had a curfew around here in months. The only thing the Doc cares about is that we are here for rounds in the mornings."

"Listen, its Happy Hour at the club tonight. How about joining us at our table? We don't invite just anybody, we are very select. How about it?" asked John. Everyone joined in.

"Okay, I'll be there, but everyone has to agree that what happened here this afternoon does not leave this room." All agreed.

"Wait a minute; how can all of you get up that hill to the club? It's really steep.

Cpt Compton and Mr. Sandusky are the only ones who can walk. Surely you don't bring the wheel chairs up that hill?"

"The Lord works in mysterious ways," John cut in. "I can assure you we will all be there."

The procession up to the club that evening looked like the remnants of Napoleon's army retreating from Moscow. Sandusky and Pete were the only ones not in a wheelchair. Between the two of them, they had two good arms. The procession went fine as long as they were in the hospital, but once outside there was a steep hill for about 100 yards up to the club.

They both doubled up on one wheelchair at a time. By the time they had gotten Jim and Childres up they had to take a rest. Pete's legs were throbbing from the unaccustomed strain.

"Jesus, I thought you SF types could walk on water. You're wasted just pushing that little old wheelchair up a little hill," said Tom.

"Listen, you Irish son of a bitch, when we get you half way up that hill, we are going to let go of you, if you don't shut up."

"Sandusky, how the hell do you think I get home from the club? I just get on top of the hill, give three warnings to anyone who might be down below, and let er rip," said Tom. "Well let's get going, I'm getting thirsty."

They put together several small tables forming a large one, which was situated in the center of the room where the bar was located.

"This is our usual setup, Pete," said John. "Gus, the bartender usually reserves a few tables for us, as you can see we need a lot of room with these wheelchairs. Of course we take care of him too, and he knows it."

They had all had a round when Pat Connor, Tom's wife, and Linda joined them.

"Pete, I see you are getting initiated into the wards happy hour. If you had waited, we could have helped you with the wheelchairs."

"We didn't have any trouble at all," said Sandusky. "Did we, guys?" Everyone concurred.

"Here comes Sandusky's latest," said Tom, nodding towards the door. The woman standing there appeared to be in her middle thirties. She was blond with her hair piled high up on top of her head.

"Oh Christ, I forgot I invited her up for happy hour," said Sandusky, getting up. "She is a new civilian nurse that got here about two weeks ago. She's great in the hay, but I have yet to touch the sides."

"Mr. Sandusky, I'm surprised at you," said Linda. "Are you sure it's her fault?"

Sandusky made a mocking move towards her as though he was about to hit her, when his friend arrived at the table.

"Here you are Freddie." Everyone at the table had trouble

keeping a straight face as Sandusky introduced her around the table. His friend, Ann, had a an extremely high pitch voice.

"I was just telling them about you when you walked up," said Sandusky, patting her on the back.

"I hope it was good, Freddie."

"Oh it was, Ann, nothing but good," said Tom. Pat gave him a jab in the ribs.

"I came up here for a drink," said Linda, "How about it?"

They all ordered a round.

"I wonder what happened to Lt Bjorkvik," said Jim. "She said she would be here."

"Well, you can't blame her for not showing, after our little session today," said Childres.

"What happened today, Tom?" Pat asked.

"Oh, nothing, nothing at all; you know how Childres is, he always says things."

"Did I hear someone mention my name," said Bjorkvik, sitting down in the only empty chair, next to Pete.

Introductions were made and Pete ordered her a drink.

"Are these guys giving you a hard time?" asked Pat.

"No, not at all, in fact they are very helpful," said Bjorkvik. "Especially with the medication."

"Not to change the subject, but I think it's your turn to play the jukebox John," said Tom.

It was a quiet happy hour. The talk centered around the buildup in VN. Bjorkvik had informed them that she was seriously thinking of volunteering to go over. They all told her it was an admirable idea.

JOHN'S STORY

John Snyder had been working on his PhD in chemistry at Yale when he decided he was tired of school. A brawny 6'4" at 230 pounds, he had played football both in high school and college, where he had acquired the nickname "animal." He found his studies boring and tedious, and decided he wanted some excitement. He applied for and received a commission of 2nd Lieutenant in the Field Artillery.

On graduation from the Basis Artillery Course at Fort Sill, he volunteered for Airborne School and for the Special Forces school at Fort Bragg, North Carolina, where he graduated at the top of his class of 100 students. His first assignment was as executive officer (XO) of an "A" Detachment consisting of 2 officers and 8 enlisted (NCO's) in the 1st SF Group in Okinawa. His detachment went through cross training where each individual on the team learned to do the job of all the other members i.e. weapons, operations, intelligence, communications, and medical. After a six month training stint in Oki, the Detachment was declared mission trained for deployment to the Republic of South Vietnam. John enjoyed his work immensely. The vigorous training had revitalized his spirit and body. His feats of strength and endurance soon became known in the SF community in Okinawa.

Arriving in the country in the fall of '64 with his team, John and his teammates were processed in at the Special Forces HQ in Nha Trang. At their briefing the team was told that they would not be going out on site to train Mercenaries, but would become part of a new special project. That was, with the exception of John, who would receive some special training and work with a few members of the Australian Special Air Service (SAS).

He had been upset at being split up from his teammates, whom he had worked so hard with. However, when he met the Australians that he would be working with, he overcame his disappointment. This three man SAS team had been training at their headquarters in Perth Australia for special missions, namely identifying VC infrastructure and eliminating them. They put John through an abbreviated course and he proved to be a fast learner. While Captain Krasnoff, the SAS leader worked primarily with John, his two Warrant Officer assistants were training two groups of 50 Nung mercenaries. These Nungs were of Chinese origin and were, on the average, about 5'9" in height, and thus towered over the average 5'4 Vietnamese.

Upon completion of their training, Cpt Krasnoff and John took their 50 Nungs and moved to the highland capitol of Ban Me Thout, in the Province of Darlac, while the two Warrant Officers and their group moved south near the town of An Loc.

John and his group took over an abandoned VN military compound on the outskirts of the city. Their gray painted trucks and camouflaged uniforms soon became known throughout the Province.

"Our first task is to tap into the existing intelligence nets in the area. Your agency, as you refer to it, is already well entrenched, and of course, is officially our boss. They have offered us their services."

"What about the VN? Is there any way to work into their nets?"

"Well, I'm rather reluctant to trust the VN, as you'll soon find out. They are too vulnerable to compromise. However, there is a little known Montagnard movement here; it's called FULRO (translated – Uniformed Front for the Liberation of Oppressed People). Their leader, Ibaham, has recently been banned from Vietnam and is now living with his army of some 10,000 in Cambodia. He is the elected leader of the 500,000 Montagnards in South Vietnam and was to have been their spokesman in the Saigon government. But again, I'm afraid the South Vietnamese leaders reneged on their promises and would not let him be seated in the government. This, as you know, resulted in the Montagnard uprising two months ago, when hundreds of VN were killed."

"If they would quit treating them as second class citizens, or savages (moi) as the VN refer to them, they could and would keep the highlands free of VC. Our SF teams have successfully trained thousands of them into highly professional mercenaries."

"Well, don't be too hard on the Vietnamese. In both of our countries we still have groups of people referred to as second class citizens. The Montagnards are 300 years behind the VN, still running around half naked, cutting the hearts or livers out of their slain enemies, depending on which of the 28 tribes they belong to, and eating them. However, they are very loyal if treated right, and once you gain their trust they are your friends for life."

"What do you think our chances are to get the FULRO to work with us?"

"I'll see what I can set up with the Agency. I have a feeling they are deeply involved with them. Meanwhile, I want you to get to know the SF "B" and "A" Detachments here in the Province. Become friendly, especially with their intelligence people."

"I'll start this afternoon."

"Okay then, I shan't see you for a few days. Take Iprang, the best Montagnard interpreter we have with you. He is a Rhade, and these are his people. Cheng can run the camp while we are gone, as I shall be doing some visiting also."

They both got up and went to make their separate preparations. John learned from the SF teams that there was a real effort being made on the part of the VC to win over the Montagnards to their cause, but had met with relatively little success. They were in the process of establishing the infrastructure of their organization, and a few of the obvious leaders had been identified.

Iprang reported that the Montagnards were reluctant to trust outsiders at the moment, especially since what happed to their leader Ibaham.

But he did learn that the Agency had supported their movement and election of Ibaham with a great deal of effort and money. The Montagnards trusted and liked the Agency people, and for obvious reasons associated the Green Berets with the Agency. However, due to the constant changeover among the Berets, they were reluctant to pass on too much information.

While John was visiting the SF camp of Boon Bring, they received word that elements of the FULRO force were about to take over the camp. They had hoisted their flag a hundred feet outside the camp perimeter. The VN SF cadre inside the camp wanted to fire on them, but the US SF advisors recommended against it. They had over 400 Montagnard mercenaries and six VN Cadre. The Montagnards were not about to fire on their own people.

The VN Cadre were afraid that the Montagnards would start slitting throats like they had two months earlier.

John and the American SF captain brought the ranking Vietnamese into the mess hall and poured him a glass of whiskey. They convinced him that if he fired on the FULRO he was dead. He reluctantly agreed.

The FULRO force came into the camp, walking in the typical Montagnard single file. They were dressed in loin cloths, black pajamas, and a variety of fatigue uniforms. Their weapons were a mixture of US World War II M-1 rifles, carbines, BAR's, and Thompson submachine guns.

They put all of the Vietnamese into the jail, a hole in the ground about six feet square with a wire mesh net over it. The Americans were placed in the mess hall. The leader of the FULRO explained that no harm would come to anyone if they did as they were told. He wanted weapons, ammunition and recruits.

They took half of the 30 caliber MG and automatic rifles (BARs) and all the ammunition they could carry. In addition, about 120 of the camp's mercenaries and their families joined them.

John tried to find out from the leader about Ibaham, if he was in good health, about the

VC situation in Cambodia, and methods of contacting them in the future should either side decide such a contact might be beneficial.

The leader, whose name was Ipham, commented only on a means of contact. He told them the Montagnards, Ibaham's force were interested in fighting the VC, that Ibaham was the true leader of all the Montagnards in South Vietnam. He could unite all of them to get rid of the VC from the Highlands in South Vietnam and the border area of Cambodia. But in order to do this he requested two things. That the US SF supply him with arms and money, and that the Montagnards be given an autonomous state in the Highlands of South Vietnam with a representative voice in the Saigon government.

John replied that he would pass on the request to his boss. At this the leader got impatient. He told them Mr. Jim already had their demands and nothing had been done. When John tried to find out who Mr. Jim was, he was told that Mr. Jim was the American who had told Ibaham to rise up and kill the VN, who were taking the tribal lands from the Montagnards and who lied to them and tricked them.

With that the leader walked out the door of the mess hall. He momentarily turned around, as if in afterthought, and told John that Mr. Jim in Ban Me Thout could easily contact Ibaham, and departed.

As soon as the FULRO force had left the area, John and Iprang departed. They got back to Ban Me Thout at dusk.

Captain Krasnoff was back when they drove into their compound. John related everything he had learned, and Cpt Krasnoff brought him up to date on his trip and information gleaned.

"It appears to me we have a very confused situation on our hands," said Cpt. Krasnoff, sucking on his pipe. "I learned basically the same thing, namely that the Agency people were spreading dissent and encouraging the Yards to rise up. However, that doesn't track with the policy as we know it. I wonder if your High Command knows about the Agency's activities regarding the Yards? That's not our job, though. Our mission is to identify the VC leaders and neutralize them one way or another."

"It would be interesting to talk to Mr. Jim. I have a feeling he is in the best position to identify the leaders."

"You're definitely right; tomorrow I want you to go over to

the SF "B" Detachment here in BMT and also to the MACV people and see if you can get a line on him. I will be spending the next few days working with two of our squads on our first elimination operation. It's the two VC tax collectors we were briefed on last week."

John spent the next morning with the SF Intelligence people. The Detachment S-2 was a Captain Insfeldt. In addition there was a Lieutenant and two Sergeants, which made up the S-2 section. None of them had heard of a Mr. Jim, or of someone whose cover name matched that.

"I'm sorry we can't help," said Cpt Insfeldt, getting up from his chair. "If we hear anything I'll let you know."

John thanked them and started to leave.

"I'll walk you to your jeep," said Cpt Insfeldt.

"You have to be careful about what you ask," he said as they reached the jeep. "I just received your clearance and mission statement from Nha Trang yesterday. Why don't you and Cpt Krasnoff meet me at Charley's warehouse three days from today? That will be Friday, at 7:30 PM; and don't eat supper that night."

"Is Charley the Chinese food merchant here in Ban Me Thout that has the food contract for all the SF camps?"

"That's right; his father runs the business and young Charley is a salesman, you might say. He is quite a playboy, has a very nice apartment above the warehouse. Most of the Americans, including the missionaries and AID people buy from them. The family is very rich, even by our standards. I'll see you there Friday night."

John had driven over to the MACV compound, which was housed in old Bo Dais hunting palace, where Teddy Roosevelt had stayed during his hunting trips to Vietnam. It was a magnificent structure consisting of two huge buildings made of teak logs in the shape of two Montagnard long houses, two stories high and connected at the second story by an arched walkway. A small PX was located on the ground floor of one of the buildings where they sold San Miguel beer. John had developed a taste for the Philippine beer while training in Nha Trang. It was rumored that General Douglas MacArthur's father had been the founder of the brewery, and the major ownership was still in the family. It was considered the best beer in Vietnam, American brands included.

John was surprised the next morning by the unexpected arrival of Cpt Krasnoff and his men. Iprang came running in and informed him of the arrival, and that there were dead. Most of the Nungs had assembled in the compound and were helping unload the dead and wounded when John arrived.

"Ran into stiffer resistance that we expected. We need some weapons training, I must say." Cpt Krasnoff looked exhausted as he briefed him on their first mission. They had reached the mess hall and John called for the cook to bring Cpt Krasnoff some refreshments. In this case it was a shot of bourbon and a cold bottle of beer, which Cpt Krasnoff downed in a few minutes.

"We have to get better intelligence. We got the people we were after but I lost three dead and five wounded out of 16 men. Much too high a ratio if we are to become effective. We need to rehearse our quick reaction tactics more."

John briefed him on their dinner engagement Friday night.

"I must say you have made some progress. If your Mr. Jim shows, ninety percent of our problems are over. A bit of good luck, eh?"

They arrived at Charley's warehouse at precisely 7:30 PM and were immediately escorted upstairs. Their jeep was driven into the warehouse and the doors closed.

Charley's apartment was a Vietnamese version of a playboy pad. Introductions were made. In addition to Charley and Cpt

Insfeldt, a Mr. Frank Forentino, who worked for the US AID mission was present. They all had a drink before dinner from Charley's well stocked bar. The conversation centered mainly on the Montagnard uprising and the formation of Ibaham's FULRO force in Cambodia.

Charley said he wanted to come over to their compound and talk to them about a possible food contract.

"You have to be very careful of Charley here," said Mr. Forentino, "He's a very sly businessman. First he invites you over for drinks and dinner, and while your guard is down he hits you for a contract. It's an old Chinese method of doing business. They figure if they give you something, you can't refuse a request from them. Isn't that right, Charley?"

Charley laughed. "You are partially correct, Frank, but I learned the method at Stanford, I'm afraid. In our practical application business course we were always taught to take potential customers to lunch or dinner, and then hit them with a subtle sales pitch when they were feeling mellow and receptive."

Everyone laughed. "It sounded better as a Chinese custom," said Mr. Forentino.

Charley's servant came in and announced that the meal was being served. They all moved into the next room where a large table had been set. Charley placed everyone around the table.

In addition to the normal dishes of rice and vegetables, there were broiled pigeons with the heads still on, shrimp, lobster and beef broiled in a soy type sauce.

"Charley, this was fantastic," said Cpt Insfeldt, pushing his chair back. Everyone agreed.

Charley accepted their compliments and told them he was always happy to have them in his humble abode, and hoped that their close association would continue. Charley led everyone back into the living area, and poured Cognac for everyone.

They were all sitting in overstuffed rattan chairs around a

circular glass top table sipping their cognac.

"Cpt Insfeldt asked that I set up this little get together," said Charley. I'm quite aware what the nature of your mission is here in the Highlands, Cpt Krasnoff. Frank and I have been working together for over three years now, and are in the position to be of some help to you."

"I know you came here hoping to meet Mr. Jim," said Frank. "But that is not possible. Things are extremely sensitive in the Highlands right now. The Montagnards are at a stage where they could easily go either way. Like Charley said, we will help you all we can. We know who the leaders are and will supply you with the names and places. Some of the leaders hold very high positions here in Ban Me Thout and in the Province of Darlac, so these eliminations will have to be handled very carefully."

"Cpt Insfeldt here has camps throughout the Darlac, Quang Duc and Tuyen Duc provinces, with excellent communication. May I recommend that we channel all information to Cpt Insfeldt and thereby making him the central collection point. Of course, a special code will have to be made up so our traffic won't be confused with his normal daily routing transmissions."

"That sounds good, Frank," said Cpt Insfeldt. "But I will have to notify my headquarters in Nha Trang that we are cooperating in this effort. Or will you take care of that through your channels, Frank?"

"I can; as a matter of fact I have to attend the weekly joint meeting at your HQ in Saigon this weekend; I will brief him then."

"I'm a little confused," said Cpt Krasnoff. "Without sounding totally ignorant, just how do you fit into this structure, Frank? Am I to assume you work for the Agency along with Charley here?"

"That's correct, Cpt Krasnoff. My cover is the US AID job. This gives me the freedom to roam throughout the highlands giving advice and support in the form of food and basic construction material to the villagers. I might add I have probably given almost as much to the VC as to our side, and I do this for a very good reason. When the people see my light green jeep with the handshake symbol on it, they let me go wherever I want and are quite open with me. They know I will help them all if they need it. So you might say I have free passage. As a matter of fact, I don't even carry a weapon. Now, Charley here was recruited by the Agency when he was in his last year at Stanford, and has been with us for over six years now. Does that answer your questions?"

"Yes, thank you, I always fee l better, you might say, when I know who I'm dealing with. John and I, of course, are under the direct control of the Agency, so in a way, you might say you and Charley are our bosses."

"Not bosses, but members of the team. Let us not meet again unless it's absolutely necessary. Although the people who saw us here tonight are trusted long time employees of mine, you can't be too safe."

"Charley is right. You will get all your information from Cpt Insfeldt here. No one will get suspicious if you and John visit the SF "B" Detachment. If for some reason we all have to get together, which I feel is unlikely, we have a safe house, completely secure, that we can utilize. Its location will be given to you when and if we need to meet."

"Are there any questions? If not, I might add on a lighter note, that if you and John are ever in the need of a rest, I would suggest a trip to Dalat. It is quite pleasant there and it so happens my father owns a very nice hotel there called the "Print House". It is secure, with our own guards and completely private."

"I recommend it highly," said Captain Insfeldt. "I have a jeep permanently parked there, available for your use. And like Charley says, the place is very private. It's a good place to relax."

"Well, I think we'd better break this up. I have enjoyed meeting you, Captain Krasnoff, John - I wish you luck; we will do our best to keep you busy. Charley, thanks for a fantastic meal."

"Thank you Frank."

They departed in five minute intervals, Captain Krasnoff and John going together. They drove along in silence until they reached their compound and the guard let them in.

"I think we are on our way," said Cpt Krasnoff, getting out of the jeep and walking toward their quarters. "Our biggest concern now is training our people."

John spent the next week working with the Nungs in quick reaction and marksmanship training, while Cpt Krasnoff worked with another group on stakeout and surveillance.

Hit men were designated, whose mission was to eliminate the intended victim while the others took care of any bodyguards he might have.

In certain cases the teams would dress in black pajamas, making them look like VC. This was usually done when it was desirable to cause confusion in the particular infrastructure. In these instances, a witness was always left alive so that he might report to others what had happened. Night ambushes were usually utilized with no survivors. After the first two months, 23 known VC leaders and a number of their bodyguards had been eliminated throughout Darlac and Tuyen Duc Provinces.

"We are only getting the small fries, John. We need to get the number one man, especially here in Darlac."

"That's going to be difficult. They are getting very cautious. It might be a good idea to take a few prisoners in this area. Perhaps we could get some information out of them."

"It might be worth a try. We couldn't bring them back here for interrogation; we would have to use one of your SF camps. I'll work out the arrangements with Cpt Insfeldt. By the way, how is our Province Chief? Any indication he might be working with the VC?"

"Nothing concrete yet. He is on the take, that we know. According to one of our contacts who works in his house, he seems to be giving away large sums of piasters to his chauffeur, which is an indicator. At first we thought he might just be paying the local bills for him, but he has a treasurer that takes care of that. On two occasions his chauffeur has been held up on Highway 21, about half way between here and Nha Trang by supposed local VC tax collectors. Each time he has been carrying large sums of money. They have never harmed him; in fact they never even took his weapon from him, which is a little fishy."

"Yes, I see what you mean. We haven't got enough on the Province Chief yet, but his chauffeur might be a good candidate. Let's observe him for the next week and then make our move if we think it warrants it. I'll go and have a chat with Cpt Insfeldt, he might have something on him."

It was mutually agreed upon to bring his chauffeur to the Boun Ea Yang SF camp located 31 kilometers east of Ban Me Thout and two kilometers south of Highway 21. The source in the house reported that the chauffeur would be driving to Nha Trang the next day, presumably on a business run for the Province Chief. The ambush was set up to look like a blockade by VC tax collectors. Cpt Krasnoff and John went directly to the SF camp to await the arrival of the snatch team and their prisoners.

Dressed in black pajamas the snatch team flagged the Province Chief's black Pugeot sedan down. The chauffeur, alone in the car pulled over and greeted the team in Vietnamese, at the same time reaching for a package on the floor of the sedan, which he handed to one of the Nungs. The chauffeur was surprised when he was told to get out of the car.

"You'd better follow your orders more carefully," he told them, "or you will be shot. You are to let me proceed as pre-arranged. In fact, you are not at the correct rendezvous; you should be 10 kilometers down the road."

One of the Nungs opened the car door and yanked him out. Another Nung jumped into the car and drove it off the road into a clump of trees where it was hidden from the road. They led the protesting chauffeur toward the SF camp and instructed him to be quiet or else.

John and Cpt Krasnoff were waiting in the camps supply house along with Iprang when the chauffeur was brought in.

"Iprang, you know what do to," said Cpt Krasnoff, indicating to John to come outside with him.

"You think he will talk?"

"I have a feeling he will. Iprang is one of the best interrogators I have ever seen."

There was much shouting coming from the supply house. Then quiet. A piercing animal-like scream emanated through the corrugated tin walls. After about 20 minutes Iprang came out. John gave him a cigarette and lit it for him.

"It's the Province Chief," he said, blowing smoke out his nostrils as he talked. "But there is more. The Province Chief is the number two man, and the treasurer for all activities in Darlac Province. Once a week he gets money from the number one man by way of a courier, and then he disperses the money through his chauffeur to the local cells.

The chauffeur says he gives out four million piasters a month, usually at a VC roadblock between here and Nha Trang. That's where he was headed when we got him today."

"Does he know who the number one man is?" asked Cpt Krasnoff.

"He says he doesn't, but I think he is lying. Should I try again?"

"Give it another go."

Iprang returned to the supply house. For a long time there were no audible sounds. Then the piercing scream again. This time more prolonged and guttural. After several more screams, silence again.

Iprang reappeared, this time with blood over the front of his shirt and hands.

"He says Chung Ho Deip is the leader."

"Christ Almighty," John said, in a whisper.

"Are you sure that's the name?" asked Cpt Krasnoff.

"You can ask him yourself, he speaks English," Iprang said with a triumphant smile on his face.

They all went into the supply house. Cpt Krasnoff and John stood to the side so the chauffeur could not see them. He was stretched out naked on his back on the dirt floor, spread eagle, with his hands and feet tied to stakes driven into the ground. His groin area was a mess of blood.

Iprang went over and stood over him, the other Nungs making room for him. He asked the chauffeur in English who the leader was.

"Chung Ho Deip, the son of the food merchant," came the weak reply.

Cpt Krasnoff and John walked out, Iprang joining them.

"Shall I dispose of him?"

"Yes, make sure his body is completely destroyed. I don't want any traces."

Without a word Iprang returned to the supply building.

"John, let's get back to Ban Me Thout. We'd better get Frank fast, and brief him on this."

As they walked toward their jeep there was a muffled shot inside the supply building. On the way out of the SF camp they stopped and thanked the SF captain for his assistance.

Frank was quiet as they briefed him on the day's happenings. When Cpt Krasnoff had finished, he took his pipe out, filled it slowly with tobacco and lit it.

"We have had our suspicions for some time. Cpt Insfeldt has been briefed on it. That's why I recommended he be the one that gave you the names. He and I have gone over each name you've been given, eliminating those we knew for sure were questionable."

"Do you want us to handle this?"

"Yes, but be careful, Charley has a couple of very dedicated bodyguards. I suggest you plan this one with extreme care. All traces will have to be gotten rid of. May I suggest you weight the bodies and fly them out over the ocean? I will see that a chopper is put at your disposal. Don't trust this one to your men alone."

"Do you think Charley's father or other members of his family are involved?" asked John.

"No, not his father, at least. He is a dedicated businessman who firmly believes in the capitalistic ways. He has a younger brother that worships him. In answer to your question, I don't know."

Frank got up and walked to the door.

"Good luck on this one. You'll need it, believe me," he said, waving his departure.

They spent the next day planning. It was decided to eliminate Charley first and then get the Province Chief. How to get Charley to a place where he would be vulnerable was the problem. All of their ideas had weaknesses in them. There was no way they could get him away from his house or business without drawing suspicion. He already had their food contract, so there was no reason to invite him over to their compound. They decided to let it ride and hope that an opportunity would present itself in the next few days before the chauffeur was missed.

Their chance arrived that very afternoon. Charley and his two bodyguards drove into their compound.

"I came to talk to you about the food contract," Charley said as he got out of his car, holding out his hand to John.

"Good to see you again," John said, shaking his hand vigorously. "Come on in and have a cold beer."

Cpt Krasnoff hid his surprise as he led Charley into their quarters. John took out the bottles of San Miguel beer from the refrigerator, and handed them out.

"I wish I could get a supply of San Miguel," said Charley, taking a long sip from the bottle.

"That shouldn't be difficult to arrange," said Cpt Krasnoff. "John, can get you a few cases at least."

"Sure, no problem. In fact, I'm going over to the PX this afternoon. I'll drop them by."

"I would appreciate that," Charley said, saluting in thanks with the bottle. "Actually, I didn't come here about the food contract. I need a favor. As you know, there have been several incidents on the road between here and Dalat, where vehicles have been blown up. We are not sure if these are VC or Montagnard-initiated incidents. I have to go to Dalat the day after tomorrow on business. What I need is the use of a plane to get there. It might be a good time for both or one of you to also go and I will show you Dalat. I will have to be back here in three days."

"I think we can arrange a helicopter for day after tomorrow. And you're right, John and I need a little relaxation. We would be delighted."

"Thank you very much; I knew I could count on you."

"We will give you the time for pick up tomorrow, as soon as a chopper is confirmed."

"Until then," said Charley, getting up and holding out his hand to them.

After Charley had departed, Cpt Krasnoff made sure there was no one else in the building. He closed the door to their quarters.

"How's that for luck," said John as Cpt Krasnoff joined him at the table which served as a planning area.

"Luck is not a strong enough word, we must be living right."

"I recommend we use the east airfield for the pickup rather than the city strip."

"I agree. Let's see, according to this map it's at least four Km from the city to the east Field. I have only been out there twice, but there is a stretch here," Cpt Krasnoff was pointing to the green area on the map, "before we get to the rubber plantation which would make an ideal ambush site."

"I concur; the problem is, how do we explain to Charley why we're using the east field rather than the city strip which is closer and where most choppers land?"

"Maybe Frank can be of some help. He has access to some graders and bulldozers. Maybe it's time the old dirt city strip was resurfaced and spruced up a bit. That would satisfy even Charley for using the east strip. Go over and see Cpt Insfeldt and have him get in touch with Frank, for both the chopper and the airfield repairs."

"What time do you want the chopper at the field?"

"Let's make it for a 10:30 pickup. The sun should be just right on the road by that time."

John had made the arrangements for the chopper and air field construction, and delivered 4 cases of San Miguel to Charley's place.

That evening and next morning was spent planning the ambush and the elimination of the bodies. It was assumed that

Charley would take at least one of his bodyguards with him to Dalat, with the other one driving them to the airfield and bringing the car back to Charley's place. So there would be three bodies to dispose of. They would only use a minimum force, Cpt Krasnoff, John, Iprang, and two others. John and Iprang would accompany the bodies aboard the chopper, weight them and dump them in the ocean.

The stretch of road they had picked for the ambush was seldom traveled, and was therefore safe for a daylight attack. John was lying on his stomach in the tall grass next to the road, his M-16 cradled in his left arm. Everything had gone so simple and easily that it worried him somewhat. His stomach was in a knot. This was the first time he had ever killed anyone he had gotten to know. He looked over at Cpt Krasnoff, about 15 feet away to his left. There was no expression on his face. Since he had known him, he had never shown any emotions whatsoever. John wondered if he ever got excited about anything. He went over the plan in his mind.

The chopper was standing by at the air field with wire and weights aboard. It was parked away from the buildings so they could approach it without arousing any suspicion. They had rehearsed the plan last night, and each man had a job. The car would be traveling at a high rate of speed. Iprang would detonate his small antitank mine at the front portion of the car, and his two assistants would fire at the tires. If the car burst into flames they would let it burn, hopefully with the victims still inside. If not, John and Cpt Krasnoff would eliminate the three people, recover their bodies and take them to the air field in their jeep.

He looked at his watch, it was 1015. Any time now. He tried to get a glimpse of Iprang and his men. They were located about 50 meters to his right. They would hit the car first. He could not see them. His hands were sweating. He wiped each of them in turn on his camouflaged shirt, insuring that his weapon did not hit the ground. He checked his selectore switch, it was on full automatic.

Insects were buzzing around his head. Touching his face to wipe the insects away, he realized a cold sweat covered his face. Christ, he was losing his nerve. These long waits were worse than the actual killing. He glanced at Cpt Krasnoff again. He was still in the same position; the only movement was his eyelids. From now on he was going to recommend they do all their jobs at night. This daylight stuff was nerve racking.

There it was! The sound of the car. He wiped his hands again and checked his weapon, making sure his magazine was firmly set. He pulled back the cocking lever and let a round slide into the chamber. He heard the car noise getting closer. He caught a glimpse of it coming around the bend.

A muffled explosion ripped the morning stillness. The front portion of the black sedan lifted into the air, still moving forward. It twisted in the air landing on the passenger side directly opposite John. He ran forward. Smoke was coming from what was left of the engine. There were no sounds. He caught a glimpse out of the corner of his eye of Iprang and his two men running toward him with their weapons at the ready. Cpt Krasnoff ran around the back of the car, firing his weapon into the gaping holes where the windows had been. John took the front, firing a burst into the front seat.

"Quickly, let's right the car so we can get at them," yelled Cpt Krasnoff. Iprang and his two men had joined them. Together they pushed and the car rolled over on its deflated tires. John yanked the front door open and Charley's body fell halfway out.

"Get the jeep," John yelled.

Iprang ran for the jeep which had been hidden down the road. He pulled Charley's body over the side of the road. Starting back, he heard a yell and firing. Cpt Krasnoff was spraying the inside of the car. Something slammed into John's right leg below the knee at the same time he hit the ground; his left foot seemed to fly into the air. The firing stopped.

"That bastard," he heard Cpt Krasnoff say.

He tried to get up but fell back. His right leg felt numb.

"Are you all right? His other bodyguard was crouched on the floor with an automatic rifle; put up quite a struggle."

"He got me good," said John in a low voice.

Iprang arrived with the jeep. Without saying a word, Cpt Krasnoff and Iprang lifted John into the front seat and threw the three dead bodies in the back. Cpt Krasnoff got behind the wheel while the others jumped on the back and side fenders. They were at the chopper in a matter of minutes. The chopper crew was ready with the rotors turning.

John felt himself getting weak. He felt hands grabbing him and lifting him aboard the chopper. Cpt Krasnoff strapped him down on the long seat in the rear of the chopper, at the same time strapping a tourniquet below his right knee and above his left ankle.

John looked to his side and saw Iprang cover the bodies with a poncho. They were airborne.

"First stop, the hospital at Nha Trang," Cpt Krasnoff shouted at him over the noise of the chopper. "You'll be all right."

He shook his head, protesting. "Dump them first." He motioned to the bodies on the floor.

"Do you think you can hold on?"

John indicated he could. Cpt Krasnoff took a small metal box which was secured to his harness and removed a small syringe. Using his knife, he cut the top portion of John's shirt-sleeve off at the shoulder. He quickly stuck the needle portion of the metallic syringe into John's shoulder, forcing the liquid into his arm.

"That should make you feel better," he shouted, sticking the empty syringe into the collar of John's shirt, bending the point of the needle so it hung from the collar.

"In case you forget to tell the docs that you already had a shot of morphine," said Cpt Krasnoff, pointing to the needle.

The morphine took effect immediately; the pain in his leg and foot subsided. He watched Cpt Krasnoff and Iprang as they tied the hands and feet of the bodies together with wire and rope and weighted them with large triangular weights.

The crew chief indicated to Cpt Krasnoff that they were over the ocean. Cpt Krasnoff made the motion for them to descend.

John tried to twist his head to look out the open door, but was unable to do so. His mouth was very dry. He tried wetting his lips but there was no moisture.

The chopper leveled off and Cpt Krasnoff gave the sign to Iprang to help him push the bodies out. As each one was clumsily pushed out the door, the chopper seemed to heave. When all three bodies were out, Cpt Krasnoff pointed to John and the crew chief nodded his head, then spoke into the small mike attached to his helmet in front of his mouth. The chopper made a sharp climbing banking turn to the left.

They arrived at the hospital chopper pad in a few minutes. An Army ambulance was standing by waiting for them. Three SF medics placed a stretcher on the floor next to John and lifted him down on to it, and carried him to the waiting ambulance.

THE PIT

It was the day before Thanksgiving and The Pit had received word that the Chief of Staff would visit them the next day.

"Oh shit." It was Sandusky who first reacted to the news.

"That means we really have to clean up this place and be good little boys."

The civilian janitors and corpsmen had taken pains in cleaning and buffing the floors. All the occupants of The Pit had to do was straighten their own personal areas, which in some cases was not an easy task.

About 10:30 on Thanksgiving Day the entourage arrived. All the visitors were in dress blues. The members of The Pit had been briefed by the hospital Adjutant, to sound off with their name, rank, and the outfit they had served with in Vietnam.

The Chief of Staff, General Johnson, walked over to Cpt Childres' bed first, which was the first bed on his left as he entered The Pit. Childres sounded off as told.

"Cpt Childres, Sir, I served with the 5th Special Forces." The Chief of Staff nodded and moved on to Jim's bed, who sounded off accordingly.

"So you were with the 1st Aviation Battalion. You men did a fine job over there. The way you fly those choppers make the American people proud of you. Good luck, Jim, I know you will come out of this all right. God bless you."

With that he moved to Pete's bed. He sounded off as directed. The C of S moved on to John's bed. Again the C of S was told his name and the unit he had served with. The Chief of Staff nodded and moved on.

At Tom's bed, he wished him God's speed and congratulated him on his fine performance in Vietnam, and how proud he personally was of the Advisory effort there. He personally knew of the hardships the Advisors suffered.

At Sandusky and George's beds, the Chief again spent several moments telling them how proud he was of them and congratulated them on a fine performance. As the Chief of Staff was about to walk out the door, John sounded off.

"Sir, General Johnson, I just wanted you to know that the

Special Forces are in Vietnam, and fighting for their lives. We had the highest attrition rate of any unit over there. In other words, we have been used, abused, and bloodied more than any unit in the history of the United States."

John's statement caused a murmur in the crowd. The Chief of Staff turned and looked at John and said, "So I have heard," and beckoned to his aide and walked out.

No one spoke. The tension was almost unbearable. It was so very obvious to everyone that the Chief of Staff had snubbed The Pit, namely those who had served with the Special Forces.

The twin doors burst open and the hospital commander's aide walked in. "The hospital commander desires that all of you remain here until he gets down here." Having said these words he quickly departed.

"I wonder what the old man has on his mind?" It was Sandusky who was the first to speak.

"Maybe he's going to tell us that the SF are really not in Vietnam, and that these wounds are self-inflicted," John chimed in.

The door swung open and Brigadier General Myers walked in with the Chief of Orthopedics, the Chief Nurse, Lt Bjorkvik, and his aide, Cpt Bushard.

"Men, I want to apologize for what happened here this morning. I can assure you though, that the Chief of Staff, General Johnson, meant no harm or slur on any unit represented here. I have come to appreciate you men in The Pit not only for your independence in taking care of each other, but for what you have done for the rest of the hospital in the building of morale. If any of you have any complaints, my door is always open to you."

Turning to his staff, he said, "I want these men left alone. I don't want any Mickey Mouse orders issued them. As far as

I'm concerned, they have total freedom of this hospital. Is that understood?"

Col Grange and Lt Bjorkvik smiled and said, "Yes sir."

Lt Col Heyden turned beat red and said, "But sir,"…..

"God dammit, I don't want any "but sir". Do you all understand?" This time the response was unanimous.

"Cpt Buchard, have you got something for these soldiers?"

"Yes sir," and with that Cpt Buchard produced two bottles of champagne, and placed them on The Pit's circular table.

"Have a good Thanksgiving, men. Having said this, the CG and his staff departed.

"Well, I'll be a son of a bitch," said Sandusky, "That old fart is all right."

"Did anyone notice Col Heyden's face when the CG issued his directives?" Tom said as he got out of bed to examine the bottles of champagne.

"I have a feeling this is only the beginning," Childres interrupted, "I have it on good authority that there is a bottle of Scotch on the way from a former Chaplain of the Army."

"Where did you get that kind of Intel - don't tell me you have friends in high places?" John laughed.

"I don't want to sound snobbish, but as some of you may know, my father is a Lt General and happens to be a good friend of Chaplain Brundage, Major General Retired. Well, he asked my father what he could do for the brave people in Ward 1. My father recommended a bottle. Old Brundage being a sipper of Scotch thought that an outstanding idea. So you see, all is not lost."

No sooner had Childres spoken the words when Lt Bjorkvik entered carrying a bottle wrapped in tissue with a red ribbon around it and a note attached.

"I have a present from an anonymous caller. He only said to enjoy it in good health."

After the famous visit, word must have spread. Besides the two bottles of champagne and the scotch, a large bouquet of flowers arrived from Former President Eisenhower and wife Mami.

The old General/Ex-President was recuperating in the hospital after a mild coronary. He had gotten the word from his private nurse that seven wounded officers, all recent returnees from Vietnam, were in the ward directly across the yard from him.

The famous gravel voiced orator of the US Senate, Senator Everett Dirksen, also paid a visit, pushed in a wheel chair by his nurse, his lap covered with a blanket. He informed the members of The Pit that he was departing for home that day and only wanted to stop by and pay his respects so such a distinguished and heralded group of young Americans. He assured them that he would see them all again in the not too distant future. As he was about to leave, he withdrew a bottle of bourbon from under his blanket and placed it on the ward table. He sincerely hoped, he said, "that the hospital officials would see fit to bend the rules so that these mightily warriors would be able to partake in the nectar of the gods, a libation so richly deserved by those who had given so much." With those words, he signaled his nurse and was summarily pushed out the door.

"Well, what do we do for an encore?" Childres said, trying to follow the Senator's progress down the corridor. "I guess everyone knows what he was in here for. He comes in about three times a year to dry out."

"I don't care what he is doing here. Anyone that brings us a bottle of bourbon like that is going to get my vote," John chimed in. "Besides, I believe a party is in order. Do I hear a dissenting vote? No one opposed? I take it then tonight we will have a party."

"Pat will be over later, I'll tell her to stop off and get some party snacks," Tom said as he wheeled himself out and down to the phone at the nurses' station.

"Dammit, I sort of wish Pat wouldn't come over so often. All she does is hover over us like a den mother."

"Listen, John, she's pretty worried about Tom. He's not out of the woods yet. That left leg of his might have to come off, too. Besides, she does a hell of a lot of favors for all of us, so let's treat her right." Having said this Childres limped off to the bathroom.

"Pete, it looks like you and I will have to get the entertainment."

"Hey, mine is coming, John, don't worry about me," Sandusky said.

"Me neither," George added.

"Well, let's get some of the nurses. Bjorkvik gets off at 3:30. She'll come. Then there is Whealen, I know she'll be here."

"Linda said she might stop by," said Jim.

"I think that's a pretty safe bet," said John, "I'm surprised you are even here."

"Pete, how about briefing the night nurse? I think it's Mrs. Foster. She'll keep uninvited visitors out of here."

By 7:30 PM things were happening. Most of the girls had arrived as predicted. Pete had talked to Mrs. Foster who was more than willing to cooperate, providing she could get a sip of that good bourbon she had heard about. A table had been borrowed from the ward's reading room and was loaded with party snacks. In addition to the liquor donated that morning, each Pit member volunteered a bottle from his bed stand. Pat had done a fantastic job in getting the snacks.

"You give us the bill for that, Pat, so we can reimburse you," said George.

"I'll give it to you in the morning. You'll appreciate it more then."

And so the party had started. Sandusky's new girl, whose name was Tracy, looked about half his age, and was wearing a loose silk dress with obviously nothing under it. Her large breasts moved like two large grapefruit every move she made. She was seated next to Sandusky on his bed, displaying a pair of well-proportioned legs.

"Hey, what do you guys think of my broad? Pretty good stuff, eh? I told you I knew women."

His talk did not seem to upset her at all. In fact, she seemed pleased, leaning over and nibbling on his ear. She was on the quiet side, but when she did say something, it was obvious that she was not the brightest of girls. It was also obvious Sandusky would not make it through the evening. He was already slurring his words and using his famous adjectives.

Linda had brought a tape deck, and soft classical music was filling the room. The only one who had not arrived yet was Bjorkvik. Pete was a little disappointed. She had promised to be there.

Everyone was enjoying themselves. The favorite topic of conversation was the morning's visit by the Chief of Staff, and the aftermath with the hospital commander and the senator.

"I would have just loved to have met that dear old Senator," said Pat. "He's from my home state, you know."

The card from the former president was passed from hand to hand.

"You know, I have a small frame which will fit that just right," said Cpt Whealen. "It would be a shame to lose it. You could hang it on the wall." All agreed it was a good idea.

Everyone was feeling good. George was tending bar with Lt Perez helping him. She looked sensational in her sweater and short skirt.

"We were just talking about you the other day, Perez," said John, "weren't we, George?"

George made a sign for John to be quiet, but Perez saw it.

"What were you talking about, George dear?" Perez said, crisply, looking at him.

"Nothing, nothing at all. I'll tell you later."

"No, tell me now. Was it good or bad, John?" Perez was starting to get angry. She was also feeling no pain.

"Listen, you bastard, you'd better not be telling war stories to your friends here."

"Hey, I haven't said a thing. I don't know what you're getting so excited about."

"You better not," she said, somewhat mollified.

"Can anyone join this party?" It was Bjorkvik.

"Come on, you're late. Everyone is at least two ahead of you. Name your poison."

Bjorkvik was wearing a form fitting knit dress that confirmed what everyone had suspected, that she had a fantastic body. She came over and sat down at the foot of Pete's bed, facing him.

"It looks like you are the only one without a partner," she said, crossing her legs. "God, this drink is strong. That George will have me drunk after a few of these." She was drinking scotch on the rocks, the same as he was.

"Listen, the other day when you came out of surgery, and I was adjusting your bed, you said a lot of things, like you wanted to take me out, and that I reminded you of your mother. Do you want me to go on?"

Laughing, Pete told her he was not responsible for anything said when he was doped up.

"Well, you did invite me to Happy Hour; told me the exact day and time to be there. I showed up but you didn't," she said good naturedly.

He apologized and assured her he would own up to all his commitments.

"You'd better," she said, sipping her drink.

They had talked about themselves and she kept him supplied with snacks and drinks. She was born and raised in Minneapolis, had attended college at the University of Minnesota majoring in nursing, and on graduating joined the Army Nurse Corps.

A loud cheer went up. Sandusky was standing on his feet. The music coming from the tape deck was the Stripper. He was gyrating with the music.

"Hey, get up," he was motioning for Tracy to join him. "Come on; let's show these folks how to really do the strip. Would you guys like to see the best looking pair of tits anywhere?" He had his hand down the front of Tracy's dress and was fondling her.

"Not here, Freddie," she laughed, moving away from him.

"Well hell, folks, if she won't, I will." He started unbuttoning his shirt.

"Attaway Sandusky, take it all off," Tom yelled.

"Oh oh, I think we are really in for a show," said Linda.

Sandusky had his shirt off and was trying to get his pants off, all the while keeping time with the music.

"Hey, I'll show you the famous flame dance," he said as he stepped out of his pants and shorts. "Help me up on the table, someone."

John put a chair by the circular pit table while Pat cleaned off the food.

"If someone walks in now we'll all go to jail," said Bjorkvik, with a desperate look on her face.

Sandusky was gyrating to the music stark naked on top of the table. "Hey, need a rolled up newspaper. The rest of the people were clapping their hands to the music and egging him on. John handed him a portion of a paper rolled up into a foot long piece. Sandusky was really getting wild on the table, almost falling off a few times.

"Hey, someone light this for me" he yelled, holding the rolled up paper towards the people watching.

"What is he going to do with it?" asked Pat.

"Just keep your eyes on old Freddie, he'll show you," said Tom.

"Hey, that's a good light," said Sandusky, holding the lighted paper in the air so everyone could see it. His next motion caused Perez to yell out. "He's crazy, he'll get burned." Everyone was clapping and yelling at him, causing him to increase his gyrations.

Sandusky had inserted the unlit end of the paper into his rectum, causing the rolled up paper to stick straight out, slowly burning its way towards his cheeks. His body was glistening with sweat and his gyrations to the music were causing the table to rock precariously.

The doors opened and Mrs. Foster walked in. "Oh my lord, I didn't see it, I didn't see it. I didn't see anything," she said, turning around and walking back out.

"My God, if anyone but Mrs. Foster had walked in I would be drummed out of the Army tomorrow," said Bjorkvik.

The music stopped and none too soon. The burning paper was starting to burn his cheeks. Sandusky jumped from the table and landed on his knees. He pulled the paper out and threw it on the floor. Tracy went to him and led him to his bed.

"Hey, I need a drink," he said. Everyone was clapping and congratulating him on his fine performance.

"We must really be getting drunk" said Whealen, taking a drink from George and handing it to Sandusky. Tracy had put his robe on him and had sat him down on the bed.

"You were really great, honey," she said, rubbing her hand around the inside of his robe.

"Well, who's next?" yelled Tom. "Come on, one of you girls."

Take it easy Tom; we're lucky we didn't get caught. We had a show, let's not press our luck," said Pat.

People were settling down after the performance.

"He is an interesting guy, old Freddie. Do you suppose there's anything he wouldn't do to attract attention?" asked Bjorkvik, handing Pete another drink.

Before he could answer, George and Perez announced their departure. Their earlier tiff must have been settled, for Perez was leading George down the hall to the side entrance.

"Sandusky's dance must have turned her on," said Tom. "I wonder if old George can handle that. I'll bet he needs a safety strap to keep from falling off. You know how hot blooded those Latins are."

"Is this a confession or hearsay?" asked Pat.

Tom was feeling no pain. "I happen to know they are not like the Vietnamese, they just lay there like a corpse, not moving. You have to do all the work. Isn't that right, guys?"

Everyone chimed in, agreeing with him.

Pete had told her about his career to date, and how he had ended up in the hospital. As he was talking, he couldn't take his eyes off her legs. She was sitting facing him at the foot of his bed; her legs crossed revealing her legs up to her thighs.

"Is there something wrong with my dress," she said, with a smile on her face. "Or do you always stare like that?"

He informed her that he always stared when he saw something he liked. She had laughed at his answer.

It was getting late and the other people were starting to disappear. Sandusky had drawn the curtains around his bed and disappeared therein along with Tracy. Pat started cleaning up the damage.

"Let me give you a hand," Bjorkvik volunteered.

They had cleaned up and were putting the bottles back in the night stands.

"You and Pete will have to sort out the liquor tomorrow," Pat informed Tom, who was having a hard time focusing his eyes.

"Well, that was a nice party. I think everyone enjoyed themselves," said Bjorkvik, "and some are still partying," pointing to Sandusky's closed curtains.

"It's about time to head home, I guess. You know, I'm great with scrambled eggs. Anyone interested?" Bjorkvik said, looking at Pete and the others.

He was kind of hungry. If she could sneak him out in his pajamas and robe, she had a date, he told her.

"Sure, come on, my car is parked outside the side entrance."

"We'll decline this time," said Pat. "Tom's too out of it to go anywhere."

He felt strange walking out in his robe.

"I don't live very far from here," she said. "Besides I don't think anyone noticed at this time of night. You know, it is after 1:00 AM."

She drove out through the gate, not saying a word. He glanced at her out of the corner of his eye. They had driven about five minutes when she pulled over.

"Well, here we are." She got out and closed her door, came around to help him out. She lived in one of the new high rise apartment buildings. Walking into the building made him feel guilty. What the hell was he doing here anyway, walking around in his pajamas and robe?

She pressed the elevator button and the doors opened immediately.

"Don't look so worried, Captain Compton, no one is up around here at this time of night."

They got off at the 8th floor. She led the way down the corridor to her apartment. She opened the door and turned on the light. "What do you think of it? Not bad for a struggling working girl, is it?"

He agreed. It was a beautiful apartment, well decorated. She kicked off her shoes and opened a small cabinet which revealed an array of bottles. "Do you want the same or something different?"

He looked at her for several moments without answering.

"Hey, what's the matter, Pete, are you scared of me?" She came toward him, and put both arms around his neck.

"Look, I'm your nurse, I know, but we can still be friends, can't we?"

He pulled her in close to him. He could feel her body pressing hard against him. He held her for what seemed a long time. Neither one spoke. He could feel her soft hair against his face. He kissed her hair gently moving around to her forehead, nose, and mouth. She returned the pressure of his lips, opening her mouth slightly. His whole body began to throb. He had not held a girl in over a year. He knew that she could feel him against her. She pulled away looking into his eyes.

"Would you like to sit down and talk for a while?"

He told her he would like that drink now. She moved over to the liquor cabinet and fixed two scotches on the rocks. She handed him one and sat down next to him on the couch.

"Would you like some eggs? It would only take a minute to fix them up."

He really didn't want any, he wasn't hungry anymore he told her. They both drank deeply from their glasses.

"You know, I'm off for the next four days. Would you like to take a drive around the city tomorrow? It really is a pretty town."

He told her that would be great. He had not been out of the ward, except for walks up to the club.

"Do you want to stay here tonight, or do you want to go back and I'll pick you up tomorrow morning?"

He looked at her and smiled, and told her that was up to

her. She put her drink down on the table.

"Don't think I go around picking up patients and seducing them. You're the first person that has been up here except for Pat Connor. But I do want you to know I have thought about you coming up here since the second day I met you."

She leaned over and kissed him gently on the lips. He pulled her close, kissing her neck and hair. He moved so she could lie on the sofa. They kissed for several minutes. He moved his hand down her legs, lifting the hem of her dress. His fingers explored the soft skin inside her thigh. She moaned softly returning his kisses in a demanding manner.

"Let's get more comfortable," she said, getting up and holding out her hand to him. They moved into the bedroom.

She kissed him on the lips and started taking off her clothes. She pulled back the covers and got into the bed.

"Hurry, Pete."

He was beside her holding her close to him. He kissed her and they both caressed each other. They made love hurriedly, she cried out when he first entered her, but joined him in the lovemaking. They lay quietly for what seemed to be a long time, both contemplating what had just transpired.

He told her he loved her very much.

"I love you too Pete, more than you can possibly realize. Next time I'll be more helpful; I just didn't know exactly what to expect. I think I'd better get up for a minute. She disappeared into the bathroom. She was a beautiful girl. They spent the weekend sightseeing and making love.

A few days after Thanksgiving, a new patient was wheeled into the "Pit." Bjorkvik reorganized the "Pit" so there would be room for him. He had a cast on his right leg up to his hip. Bjorkvik got him settled. "This is Lt Ramos," she announced to the "Pit" members, "Newly arrived from Vietnam."

"I need a shot of Demerol right now," Lt Ramos said.

Bjorkvik explained to him that the Dr. had prescribed Darvon pills. Lt Ramos let Bjorkvik know in no uncertain terms that he was not an ordinary patient and that he wanted to talk to the Dr. Bjorkvik kept her cool and said she would talk to the Dr. Lt Ramos also wanted a phone right now so he could call home.

"Give me the damn Darvons. It will probably be an hour before the doctor gets here." Bjorkvik gave him the Darvons and walked towards the door. The "Pit" members could tell she was agitated.

"Anything we can do?" asked John.

Bjorkvik merely held up her hand and indicated for them to leave her alone as she departed the "Pit."

A Red Cross lady carrying a phone arrived about ten minutes later. She pulled the curtains around the bed and plugged in the phone and told Lt Ramos he could make his call. Within about five minutes, there was loud shouting behind the curtains, but it was not in English.

Childres walked over to the curtains and listened. He whispered that it was Spanish – maybe Puerto Rican. Lt Ramos was on the phone for about a half hour. Dr. Berg came in with Bjorkvik and went behind the curtains. He sounded stern and informed Lt Ramos that he would not tolerate abusive language to his nurses and he might get a shot of Demerol to make him sleep tonight. With that, Dr. Berg opened the curtains and introduced Ramos to each of the "Pit" members.

John asked him what unit he had been with.

"The 1st Cav Air Mobil," had been the short trite answer.

"Were you with Hal Moore's outfit in the Idrang Valley?" asked Childres.

"Yes, of course, who else has been in the Idrang Valley?" challenged Lt Ramos.

"Well, we have two people here who have spent some time there," replied Childres in an even tone.

"Well, I'm not interested," said Ramos and turned his head saying he was tired.

The next afternoon, a group of about 20 visitors were escorted into the "Pit" by Bjorkvik. They surrounded Ramos' bed and hugged him and started asking questions. All of a sudden, an elderly woman started shouting in Spanish at Ramos.

Most of the "Pit" members were seated around the "Pit" table and Childres was trying his best to translate in a quiet voice. "Evidently, Ramos had told his family on the phone yesterday that he had lost both legs and the doctors were not sure he was going to survive. His father had chartered a jet to fly the family up here, and now the grandmother is giving Ramos hell for scaring the family when all he got was a bullet in his butt!"

The "Pit" members looked at each other, and it was decided that if Dr. Berg did not send Ramos to another room they would request it.

Three days later Ramos was gone. No one asked where.

John took the call. It was Johnny Ireland. He invited John and some of the ward members to be the guests of the football team for the coming weekend. Johnny Ireland owned a club downtown where the Football players hung out, called "Little Bit of Ireland." It was not certain who had adopted whom. Whenever the players were strapped for cash or other favors, Johnny always took care of them. He knew everyone and could always be counted on for a favor regardless of its nature.

Some of the ward members had frequented his establishment and had gotten to know him well. John knew better than to turn him down, and promised to get some of the guys and bring them down Saturday night. Walking back into The Pit, John announced the invitation.

"It looks to me like a bachelor setup; who's interested?"

No one spoke. "Well, how about it? The football team

promised us a good time. Do I have any takers? How about you, Jim?"

"No thanks, I don't think Linda would understand."

"I don't think Linda would understand. What kind of crap is that? You aren't married to that broad. Boy, has she got you by the short hairs."

"What about you Pete? You haven't been out in a while. Let's me and you have some fun this weekend. I can guarantee it, if Johnny is involved it's going to be a pisser."

He had told John it sounded great and that he was game. He certainly didn't have any commitments to anyone. Bjorkvik had been cool since their first and last encounter at Thanksgiving. It would be good to get out.

"If I thought I could get away with it, I'd join you guys. But I have pissed Pat off too much lately to press my luck. I'll tell you what, I'll go down to Johnny's for a few drinks, though."

"Great, Tom," said John, "I think the plan is to tip a few down there and then proceed to bigger and better things. You can stay and chew the fat with Johnny after we leave. You two Irishmen get along great anyway, telling all those lies."

It was agreed upon to keep the whole thing low key. There was to be no mention of it to anyone, especially wives and girlfriends.

"We'd better keep it from Bjorkvik also," said Tom. "Her and Pat are getting together quite often these days. In fact, too much. I have a feeling they are cooking something up, and my gut tells me the main course is poor Pete here. He's the most eligible bachelor around here."

He told them not to worry about him and Bjorkvik as there was nothing going on. He had only been out with her that one weekend.

"We hear you pal, but let's keep this under our hats," said Tom.

They took a cab to Johnny's place. It was only 6:00 PM but already it was crowded. Johnny spotted them as they entered and motioned for them to go to the back room. Making their way to the back, several of the steady customers recognized Tom. Offers of drinks were made, but politely refused.

"I must be crazy to turn down free drinks," mumbled Tom as they reached the back room. It was partially partitioned off from the main room. There was a smaller bar and the tables were long rectangular with benches. It was intended to be a place where private parties could be held, but due to the popularity of the place, it ended up taking the overflow.

Walking into the room they were greeted by several of the football players. Introductions were made. John informed them that Tom would not be staying with them, and that he and Pete would be the only participants.

"Well, let me tell you what we have planned," said Sam, who was the spokesman. "We figured you guys were probably going stir crazy by now. Although from what I hear through rumor control, you aren't exactly bored up there. Anyway, we'll do a little drinking and club hopping. They have a new act down at the Silver Slipper, which you might enjoy. Maybe after that, something to eat, and then over to Bill's place here for a few games of alligator."

The other members of the team chuckled at the mention of alligator.

"Should we explain to our war heroes here what alligator is all about, or should we wait?" asked Bill.

It was a unanimous decision to wait.

"Hey, since I won't be participating, I think it's only fair to tell me," said Tom.

Sam took Tom over to the bar, and explained the game rules. I don't believe it," was all Tom said as he came back to the table.

"Believe it, my friend, believe it," said Bill.

"Well, that will work out just right. We have 11 girls joining us, so the nine of us and you and Pete works great. Hey, we're doing a lot of talking and not much drinking," said Sam. "Barkeep, another round of our special. I think you'll like this. All I'm going to tell you is that the base is vodka and the drink is chilled to almost freezing. We've found that you are able to drink more and longer and stay relatively sober on this. Johnny makes the stuff up ahead of time for us."

"This is really great," said Tom. "It's sort of dry, not sweet like so many vodka drinks usually are."

They sat around and talked. The season had just ended for them, so they didn't have to worry about training.

"The people around this table are all old regulars and have been together for about four years," said Bill.

"Old is right." Johnny had joined them. "These guys are getting so old they can collect social security. All you have to do is to watch them play on Sundays and you'll see what I mean."

Some of the guys pounded Johnny good naturedly on the head and shoulders referring to him as the innkeeper of a true Irish whorehouse.

"Well, you guys should know," quipped Johnny. "By the way, is everything set for tonight?"

"Yah, everything is set. We'll be at Bill's place about 12:30," said Sam.

"That's a good time. Don't forget to take them over to Leon's place, also. He would be insulted if you didn't. He's been wanting to do something for these guys for a long time," said Johnny, taking a sip from his drink.

"Good idea, they can then see our city's finest in action," said Bill.

After another round of drinks, it was decided to start hitting a few places. Tom stayed with Johnny. The rest of them split up into three cars and started for the next place.

They were on their way to Leon's with everyone in good spirits. The places they had been to so far all had the girlie shows with the routine strip acts.

"I think the next place will impress you," said Sam. "As you'll see it doesn't look like a club, and entrance is by invitation only. In fact, we might as well eat here, old Leon serves about the best food in town, besides the best girls."

Leon's was located in what had been an old mansion. There were no signs, other than a small brass plate by the door bell, with the word Leon inscribed on it.

Sam rang the bell. A doorman answered, and before Sam could say anything the doorman told them to come in, and that Mr. Leon was expecting them.

"We would like to get some dinner first," said Sam.

The doorman told them to follow him, leading them down the stairs to what appeared to be a basement. A heavy wooden door opened and revealed a paneled dining room. There were no tables as such, only semi-private booths.

The first thing Pete noticed was that the waitresses wore transparent blouses. The doorman led them to a large booth and closed the semi-transparent curtains. "The reason they close us in like this is so no one can see who is in the other booths," said Sam. "This is where the prominent people of the city hide out from their wives and husbands."

A waitress brought them complimentary cocktails and took their orders.

"I'd like to get a little of that," said John. "I haven't seen a pair of beauties like that in a long time."

"Take it easy, my friend, there are plenty of those around," said Bill.

A different waitress brought them their orders. "Mr. Leon says to enjoy your meal and he will see you all on the second floor when you have finished. If you need anything else please let me know."

"I can't believe this place," said John, cutting into his prime rib.

The second floor proved to be something out of playboy magazine. Mr. Leon escorted them to three separate tables. Sam made the introductions.

"If there is anything we can do for you let me know. If there is anything, anything at all let me know." Mr. Leon bade them farewell and departed.

"He means that," said Sam, "Anything at all means anything at all."

"This must be the fanciest whorehouse in town," said John.

The stage lit up and two girls were starting a routine. All the waitresses were topless and it was hard to decide just where to look. The two girls on stage were now stripped down to their shoes and were into a lesbian routine.

"Jesus, this is like Saigon or Mexico," said John. "I can't believe a show like that here."

They were on their 2nd round of drinks when Sam announced that it was time to go. They said goodbye to Mr. Leon and thanked him for his hospitality. Pete was getting drunk and he realized it. On the way to Bill's place all he could think of was Bjorkvik. He was wishing that he had made a date with her instead of going with John.

They arrived at Bill's apartment. It was huge with three bedrooms, and a large living room dining room combination. Everyone was half drunk. Bill produced a large frosted pitcher of the vodka concoction and everyone cheered, getting in line for their share. The doorbell rang, and Sam opened the door and greeted the girls.

"Come on in and have a drink, we're way ahead of you." Sam made the introductions. They were all friendly and congenial. Pete was talking to a brunette who said she worked for a Congressman. She informed him that all of the girls but two were employed by either Senators or Congressman, the other two worked in the front office for the general manager of the team.

It was obvious that they all knew each other. Sam told them about Pete and John being Green Berets and heroes of the Vietnamese war. Most of the stuff he told them were lies, but they seemed to believe him and made a big fuss over them.

After everyone had had a drink, Sam announced that it was time to liven things up a little. He instructed all the girls to go into one of the bedrooms and the guys in the other bedroom. He and Bill closed all the drapes so that no light from the outside came in. They checked the room by turning off the lights to see if it was dark enough. When they were satisfied they joined the guys in the bedroom and announced that all was ready.

"Here are the rules of the game," Sam said, turning to John and Pete. "We all get undressed in here. The girls are doing the same in the other room. We have turned off all the lights in the living room, so that it is pitch black in there. We all meet in there and grab a partner. However, there is a catch. You have to crawl like an alligator, hence the name of the game. The girls will do the same. Any questions?" There were none. "John you can improvise if you have a problem with your leg."

"I can't believe this," whispered John, as he was getting his clothes off.

The lights were turned off, the door opened, and they crawled into the next room. It soon became obvious that the girls were already there. There was some squealing and giggling.

Pete crawled forward toward where he thought the windows were. He had gone about ten feel when his hand touched a naked back. He grabbed the naked body and pulled her to him. She giggled and whispered, "We can't do it that way, it has to be alligator style," and rolled over on her stomach again.

There were some small screams and muffled laughter through the room. He heard John curse. It sounded like he was across the room from him. Pete by now was aroused and got on the girl's back. She spread her legs and helped guide him.

"Oh God," she half moaned and whispered as he went inside her. She helped him all she could and after a few minutes it became obvious that she had had enough. She made a moaning sound and flattened out on the carpet. He lay on top of her still hard inside of her. The sounds throughout the room had now subsided. Pete got off her and lay alongside of her.

"My God, are all you green berets like this?" she whispered, taking him in her hand. He asked her quietly how she knew who he was.

"Listen, I've been with most of these guys and they are not very good," she whispered.

She pulled him toward her and rolled over on her back. They made love again, this time more gently and slowly.

"You and I need to get together again. Why don't you come over to my apartment later? Everyone will pair up and disappear after a while. We'll switch partners in a few seconds. I'm Joy, by the way. See you later."

"Okay, it's time to find another partner," yelled Sam.

The same routine took place three more times. Pete's knees were getting sore and his arm was hurting. He was lying next to one of the girls he had been talking to earlier when the lights switched quickly on and off.

The game of alligators was over. There was some complaining and also some sighs of relief as they started heading back to their respective bedrooms.

"Can you believe this?" John said to Pete. "I have read about these kind of parties, but never expected to participate in one. By the way, I have a date for after. How about you?"

He told John he also had had a proposal but was not certain he could take anymore.

"I know how you feel, but I figure I'm going to make it last as long as possible. After all, I don't want to appear ungrateful."

Pete had gone home with Joy and had ended up in bed again. He and John had both gotten back to The Pit the next afternoon within half an hour of each other. They had both gone directly to bed without talking to anyone.

"Hey, what's the matter with those two?" said Jim. "They walk in here at five in the afternoon and don't say a word about last night to anyone."

"I think their silence and the fact that they are sound asleep tells it all," said Childres. "Let's leave them alone."

"Well, I see our two adventurers are back," said Bjorkvik, walking into the room. She walked over to Pete's bed and shook him gently.

"I just want to remind you, Cpt Compton, that you have a full schedule of lab tests first thing in the morning," she said in a sarcastic tone.

Pete was awake immediately. He sat up rubbing his eyes in disbelief.

"Pat told me. Tom came home stoned last night and told everything," she whispered. Tears were welling up in her eyes. "I came over to pick you up yesterday and have you over for dinner, but you had already left. I guess I had it coming. I haven't been very friendly lately." Tears were now running down her cheeks. "I'm sorry I'm making a fool of myself."

He asked her if she still had something to eat at her apartment. She nodded her head.

He told her it would take him two minutes to get dressed, and that he would meet her by the side entrance. Bjorkvik got up and walked out of the room.

Neither one spoke on the way over to her apartment. Once inside she asked him if he wanted a drink. He indicated yes and sat down on the couch. He watched her as she fixed the drinks and brought them over to him, sitting down next to him.

"I'm sorry about the scene in The Pit, I had no right to act like that. We have never had an understanding of any sort and we are both free to do as we please." She paused to take a sip of her drink. "It's not easy for me to go to bed with anyone, and as you very well know, you were the first. I thought that weekend meant something to you, but I guess men are different. I really love you a lot, Pete. The reason I haven't seemed overfriendly was because I was afraid you would think I was trying to trap you. When Pat told me about last night, I was really hurt."

He leaned over and kissed her gently on the lips, and asked her where his dinner was.

It was the first Sunday in the New Year and all the members of The Pit were back from their holiday leaves. Of the seven members, only Tom and Pat had stayed in town, everyone else had departed for their homes and families. The war in Vietnam was getting bigger and better, and it looked like some of The Pit members would get another crack at it if it continued at its present rate. Most of the TV news commentators were optimistic about an imminent surrender by the Viet Cong, now that the US had three regular Army Divisions there.

They did mention though, that there were still a lot of rumors among the fighting men that the VC were using Cambodia as a sanctuary, and the Regular North Vietnamese troops had entered the war, shelling US positions along the South Vietnamese border.

One American three star general had said when asked about this situation by the newsmen, "Hell, yes, they're shooting the shit out of us over there, and we can't do a thing about it.

Politics, you know." He later had to go before the cameras and retract his statement, and as a news commentator reported, the general was transferred to Hawaii soon thereafter.

"Can you believe that horseshit?" It was John commenting on the news. "We have pictures, taken prisoners, and have sent in hundreds of reports. What the hell were all those cross border operation for that the SF have been conducting for the last two years? Not to mention all the personnel we have lost, conducting those operations. This whole goddamn situation is starting to stink. No wonder there is an undercurrent of dissent starting all across this country. By the way, Pete, which side of the border were you on when you caught it? Never mind….."

"Hey, speaking of operations, do you guys realize that everyone except Sandusky is scheduled for major surgery next week? That reminds me, Sandusky, the Officer of the Day (OD) came by while you were out. It seems you came down on report for being drunk last night in the main lobby. The OD was really pissed."

"Oh, that fucking faggot, he doesn't know what he's talking about. I merely walked through there."

"Not according to him you didn't. You called everyone names up there, and propositioned an old lady in a wheelchair. To top it off you pulled your famous stunt of puking all over the couch and carpet. Now that's the kind of shit that's going to get us all in hot water, not to mention ruining our setup down here. The OD went to bat for you and calmed the people down. The only reason he knew it was you was because you also told them that you were from The Pit."

"Okay, I'll talk to him and apologize. You guys satisfied?"

For the next few days everyone was busy getting lab tests taken and appearing before post-ops boards. These boards were merely a group of doctors who evaluated the patient's progress to date, and discussed the best course of action to be taken next.

It was sort of like Grand rounds, except the patient went to the doctors. In many cases, well known civilian specialists were called in for consultations and to offer opinions on procedures.

As Pete sat there in front listening to them, a sense of security and confidence enveloped him. They were looking at the latest x-rays, pointing out things which he was unable to see or understand. It was truly a professional group of people, and he felt completely safe and knew whatever they decided would be the right thing to do. As he was being dismissed and walking toward the door, Col Grange asked him, "Everything all right down in The Pit? I hear some strange things once in a while. Maybe it's a good thing we're taking you guys out of circulation for a while. It will give the nurses and ODs a break."

He had answered that everything was fine and that incident with the OD had been taken care of.

"I knew you guys would handle it," Col Grange said with a smile.

As he walked back to The Pit, Pete kept thinking that there had to be a way to control Sandusky, or maybe slow him down a bit. He would talk it over with the others.

Tuesday they got the word from the anesthesiologist: no drinking or eating after midnight. This was the standard procedure prior to surgery. That evening everyone was quieter than usual, each one thinking about the next day. Both Tom and John were scheduled for resections. The procedure entailed cutting back about an inch off their stumps and sewing the skin over the bone so it would heal, and could eventually be able to be fitted with a prosthesis.

George and Childres had tendons in their lower legs which had to be freed from scar tissue which had formed as a result of their wounds.

Jim was to have the final operation on his hand, which included the removal of two of his knuckles. They were, in actuality, only splintered bone stubs.

His own operation involved the grafting of bone from his hip to his hand. Actually, they were taking a chunk of bone out of his iliac crest and inserting it into his lower hand, a procedure which promised to be quite painful for the first two or three days after surgery, according to the doctors.

Everyone seemed to be coming along pretty well, mentally. That is, getting over what had happened to them and starting to make plans for their future.

Tom was the only one who had made up his mind to get out of the service. He figured with his disability, the Army would pay him quite generously for the rest of his life. Besides, he had plans to go into the wood processing business with his father.

Jim was the slowest in coming around, but was in an upbeat mood after he had been presented the Purple Heart. He had maintained that his chopper had been hit by ground fire and the SF Cpt had confirmed it.

Aside from the medal aspect, perhaps what weighted most on his mind was thinking about going through the rest of his life with only one good hand. To him, it was a form of advertisement that he was not a complete human being. Many lengthy discussions by The Pit members had taken place as to what they would do if they were in Jim's shoes, each one offering his opinion. The unanimous conclusion had been reached that if a person had to lose anything, the foot or lower leg would be better, and most readily accepted by society.

This, of course, had not helped Jim any, who had reluctantly agreed. Even Linda was not able to snap him out of it. It was the standard procedure in The Pit that if anyone was in a funk, or felt down, the others did their best to cheer him up or get his mind off his problems. This was often in the form of insults, or asking the individual to perform some personal task for them. This worked in most cases.

Of all The Pit members, Tom was potentially the most serious problem. In addition to his right leg, which was cut off above the knee his left leg had developed osteomyelitis, which could eventually result in the removal of the entire leg. The doctors felt that it had been arrested, but only time would tell.

TOM'S STORY

Tom Connor had been assigned to MACV as an advisor in April of 1964. However he had been detailed to work with the Agency in the northern portion of Vietnam known as I Corps. The office he worked out of was located in Tam Key. His job cover was that of an advisor, wearing a uniform and assigned to the Province Headquarters. It was easier and less obtrusive to travel around in a uniform as opposed to civilian clothing, which immediately pinpointed one as an AID official, Agency or police advisor. Tom lived in a villa which he shared with four other legitimate advisors and his boss, Bert Kramer, head of the Agency office for the area. Most of Tom's job consisted of gathering intelligence and was usually done in the form of dead drops, which meant he never actually saw or made personal contact with the agents or plants, but rather picked the information up from a prearranged place. This was an old and commonly utilized method; thus in case of capture or compromise, the agent never knew who his contact was and could not divulge any real information on the actual intelligence setup. He had participated in several insurgences into North VN; this had been done in conjunction with the Navy.

Tom had been sitting on the porch of the villa one Saturday afternoon, sipping a beer and watching the guard at the entrance to the villa. Guards had been hired by the Agency to watch over the villa and make sure no one tampered with the vehicles. There had been several incidents in which grenades had been thrown into places frequented by US personnel, or their vehicles sabotaged.

It was September and the weather was pleasant in the northern part of Vietnam. He had six more months to go on his tour and was looking forward to going home and living like a real person again. It was also time for him and Pat to think about starting a family. His thoughts were interrupted by Bert Kramer's pulling into the driveway in his light green jeep. Jumping out, he motioned for Tom to follow him into the villa. Reluctantly Tom walked into the back room occupied by Bert.

"Close the door Tom, and sit down. I'm afraid we've got a hot one on our hands." When Bert said they had a hot one, Tom had learned that it usually meant that he had a lousy job waiting for him, not Bert.

"One of our Grey Ghosts, a C-123 aircraft, went down with 25 people aboard." Bert took a deep drag on his cigarette before continuing. "Actually there were 25 plus the plane's crew of four. All the personnel were rigged for jumping. The plane has been located by one of our Blackbirds in the Tri-border area. It looks like all aboard are dead."

"Is it part of the Yankee operation, or some other project?" asked Tom, somewhat puzzled, for usually he would not be briefed on these types of missions, although he was familiar with them.

"No, it's the old Leprechaun project, which as you know is our most extensive operation north of the border. We were trying for an insertion in the northern plateau area where we've had favorable reception from the Maroong Montagnards."

The crash of the C-123 no markings on the fuselage painted either black or dark grey depending on availability was used for cross border operations. In this case covert operations were tried to establish viable opposition in the North utilizing local Montagnards as mercenaries which had proved so successful in the south, but it never really became a success in the North despite numerous attempts.

"What has this got to do with us?" asked Tom, somewhat confused.

"We have to go in and get the codes and destroy the remains of the people and the plane. As a matter of fact, you have been tapped for the assignment." Bert sat back and waited for the reaction he knew was forthcoming.

"What the hell am I supposed to do? I don't know where the codes are, and how am I supposed to get in there? What the hell do we have all those high paid Special Forces teams for – to put on demonstrations for visiting firemen?"

"You won't be going in alone. Engles will be going with you, he knows who has the codes and can identify them. He's waiting for you at our airstrip up north. The plane was flying the nape of the earth and apparently crashed into one of the mountains. You know the procedure, it flies low to avoid radar and then pops up to jump altitude and then down on the deck again."

"Just how am I supposed to get in and get this stuff out, or shouldn't I ask?"

"We can't risk a chopper, they're too noisy. You'll have to jump in."

Tom started to get to his feet but changed his mind. "Jump! Are you crazy? I've never jumped out of a plane in my life. Do I get a week's training or what?"

"You leave in a few minutes for the airstrip up north. I have a plane waiting for you now to take you up there. Engles will give you a few pointers about the chute and how to land. You have to go in tonight, during semi-dark conditions. " Tom let out a sigh. "I still don't understand why we don't let the SF do this, it's their bag."

"Tom, as you know, a few of their people are working with us, but we're trying to keep this close hold so there won't be any leaks to the press."

"Am I correct in assuming that all the dead aboard are sterile? And by the way, what nationality are they, indigenous, Americans, or what?"

"The crew is from Taiwan, there are two US and the rest are indigenous."

"Will I be able to identify the US or have they been to our charm school?"

"You won't be able to identify anyone. Anyway that is of no concern. When you have gotten the codes, I want you to destroy the plane by using some of our magnetic devices on the exterior wing tanks to blow it with."

"What happens if we get into trouble?"

"We have a Special Forces reaction force standing by at Hue Fuby, at their animal farm up there. Engles has the rest of the information, so get going."

Tom got up and went to his room, where he grabbed his rifle and rucksack which was always ready and packed, and headed out the door.

"Tom, the reason you were picked was because I knew you would get back one way or another."

Tom slammed the door and walked over to his jeep and threw the rucksack into it. The guard indicated to him that the jeep was all right. He headed out to the airfield, driving the jeep as fast as it would go. How the hell had he gotten himself into this crap anyway? Why didn't he serve his time like everyone else? Jumping out of a plane. That's why he had gone into the Armor branch, where they didn't require all that airborne, ranger shit. All they wanted was for their officers to be good tankers. He saw the Air America plane sitting by the Operations Center. It was no secret that Air America was owned and operated by the Agency. He went inside the small operations building and greeted the Vietnamese in their own language. There was a tall lanky American standing in the corner.

"Captain Connor, I'm your pilot," he said, reaching his hand out.

Taking his hand, Tom said in a sarcastic voice, "Let's get going, I wouldn't want to miss out on this." Walking out the door, he told the Vietnamese to take care of his jeep.

They walked over to the plane, a single engine turbo-prop Swiss made Porter. It was a passenger craft, and could take off in about 200 feet and land in less.

"Climb in, she's all ready," said the pilot.

Tom strapped himself in the co-pilot's seat and sat back and relaxed. They took off going almost straight up, and leveled off at 2000 feet. It would take a little over an hour to reach the Agency's strip at Hue Fubi. He tried to close his eyes and relax, but the thought of jumping out of a plane made a knot in his stomach. He knew that he probably should be worried about what could possibly happen once they got on the ground. If the plane was as close to the border as Bert had indicated, it would be just a matter of time before the North Vietnamese discovered the wreckage. Looking down he recognized the countryside and noticed that they had started their descent. Engles, who he knew from previous operations and was truly an expert in covert operations, was waiting for them as they landed. Engles had been with the Agency since the Korean Conflict, and was renown both within and out of the Agency circles.

"Hi Tom, nice to see you again," Engles said, holding out his hand. They walked over to a hangar on the opposite side of the airfield.

"I suppose Bert has filled you in on the operation. I hope you don't mind but it was me who requested you personally." Tom made a face and gave him the finger.

"I know, you can't stand anyone who is not a jumper. You told me as much last time I saw you, although you were a little plowed, as I remember," Tom said mockingly.

"Well, let's get on with it, Tom. It's really quite simple." Engles demonstrated a few jumps off the various platforms, emphasizing what to watch out for and what not to do. Tom went through a few jumps. It didn't seem too hard. Next Engles explained how a parachute worked. A chute hung suspended from the ceiling of the hangar. He had been strapped into it and elevated so that he hung a few feet off the ground. When they had gone through all the procedures, Engles asked if he had any questions.

"Yeah, one. How do I get out of this outfit and back to normal soldiering?"

"Don't worry, we'll make out all right. Let's go and check our weapons and the demo kits."

They had gone through their equipment checklist and had taken a backup for everything, except for their weapons.

"We have about 4 hours to kill. Let's go and have something to eat and drink; our mess is serving some real fine chow these days."

It was already dusk as they were getting their chutes on before boarding the plane, assisted by some of the Agency personnel. The parachute proved to be quite bulky and uncomfortable.

The straps were digging into him everywhere. He was going to be glad when it was finally over. Their equipment bags were strapped to their fronts under the quick release device, and the weapons along their sides.

"I just thought of something," said Tom. "How do we get out once we have the codes?"

"I was wondering when you would ask. If we go in and don't run into any unfriendlies, we take a heading of 174 degrees on our compass and start walking until we get to the edge of the forested area, which as you know ends abruptly in that area, and becomes a wide grassy plain for the next 10 or 20 kilometers. We turn on the beacon portion of our radios and wait for our pickups which should be on station by 0600 tomorrow. What that means is that we have a lot of ground to cover tonight. You know the SOP in case either one of us gets wounded and can't travel."

"Yah, I know. By the way, I don't have any pills, or morphine for that matter."

"The green kit I gave you has everything you need."

The static lines from their chutes were hooked on to D rings on the floor of the plane so that when they went out the chutes would open automatically. The plane started moving down the runway and made a steep climb to the right. The knot in The Pit of his stomach was getting worse. Flight time was a little over an hour.

"Oh, by the way, we will be going out at 400 feet instead of the normal 1200 feet," Engles shouted at him. "That way there won't be so much drift and we'll land closer to the target."

This last bit of news jarred Tom's stomach some more. What the fuck was he doing here? This was absolutely the last time he would go along on one of these hair brained schemes. He started going over in his mind exactly what he had to do and the emergency procedures in case anything went wrong. He had the frequency memorized. The more he thought about it the more nervous he got. Where the hell would he land? You couldn't see anything in the dark. They could be waiting for them once they hit the ground and blow their shit away. That's probably why they had picked him instead of a well-trained agent who they had invested a lot of time and money to train. He felt a jab in his arm. It was Engles telling him they had five minutes to drop time. Christ, it seemed like they had just taken off. Could it really be that close? He told himself to relax and be calm and not to work himself into a state. He tried looking out the window in back of him, but all he could see was darkness.

"Check your equipment, and get ready," Engles yelled at him. The plane took a sudden dive, causing him to get a sickening sensation in The Pit of his stomach. At first he thought they had been hit, but then remembered the jump altitude. Engles moved to the open door and sat on the floor. He motioned for Tom to move down next to him. The cool wind hitting Engles' face caused it to look distorted, as the pilot had not slowed the plane down to jump speed yet. The full force of the prop blast was making it hard to hang on to the floor mountings. The co-pilot leaned back and yelled the 30 second warning. Tom's stomach felt like he was going to throw up. The chute straps were digging into his groin. He saw the hand of the co-pilot hit Engles on the head and the next instant he watched Engles shove himself forward and disappear into the darkness. He immediately pushed off and felt the wind blast hit his body, twisting it sideways. A sudden jerk stopped him as the parachute blossomed above him. He started to get his composure back and started thinking about what to do next. The dark ground seemed to be rushing up at him. Before he could think of landing he was coming down amongst the trees. Branches hit him and tore at him as he slid down the side of the tree. He felt the chute momentarily catch on a branch, which almost stopped him in mid-air. He heard something tear and his next realization was that of hitting the ground. He laid without moving for a few seconds, checking his body to make sure everything was all right. Getting stiffly to his feet, he removed the chute and folded it up, placing it under some bushes. He was getting his gear together when the thought hit him. Where the hell was Engles! He couldn't yell. He had not seen Engles as he descended. Oh shit! Here he was in the middle of nowhere and had forgotten what Engles had told him about looking out on the descent for the plane and for him.

"Are you all right?" It was a whisper to his rear. Engles appeared out of nowhere.

"Shit, am I glad to see you," Tom said in a whisper.

"Okay, let's go. I spotted the plane, it's only a few yards away."

They started making their way quietly through the dense undergrowth. They had only gone a few hundred meters when Engles pointed to his left. Tom could barely see the outline of the tail portion of the plane.

"Let's get a little closer and then you cover me. I'll go in and take a look." Engles moved forward and was about 30 feet from the plane. Tom moved up and joined him.

"Let's just watch it for a few minutes to make sure there is no one around."

It was eerie watching the plane, knowing there were bodies inside. They waited ten minutes, then Engles indicated he was moving in. Tom made sure the safety was off and the magazine firmly in place on his rifle. The rear door of the plane had opened on impact. The left wing was partially torn off. It was amazing, he thought, that it had not burst into flames. He saw Engles reappearing from the plane and coming toward him.

"I need your flashlight, mine's broken." Tom gave him his light and Engles entered the plane again. He could see the illumination from the light inside the plane. Engles reappeared again carrying a small packet in his hand.

"Here, stick this inside your shirt," he told Tom, handing him the packet. Tom did as he was told.

"Now let's rig this bird and blow it. You take the right side and wing tank and I'll get the left side."

Tom moved to his destination and attached the magnetic devices to the wing tank and set the timing device. He also planted one where the wing and fuselage were joined and one to the bottom of the plane. Moving to the back of the plane, he saw Engles planting his last device, and started moving toward him.

"You move to the back and into the bushes, I want to take one more look inside. It looks like they all bought it, but I want to make sure." Engles moved to the entrance of the plane and disappeared inside. Tom moved to where he could observe the entrance and still be hidden from any observers. Engles was taking a long time. The plane was set to blow in thirty minutes. Finally he saw Engles reappear, at the same time he heard noises to his left, and a burst of MG fire hitting the side of the plane and Engles' body twitching. A heavy volume of MG fire hit the plane continually for about 15 seconds, raking Engle's body, now lying half in and half out of the plane.

Tom lowered himself and started moving away from the plane and in the direction they had come. He now heard voices all around the plane. They were VC, he thought, they didn't have the distinct North Vietnamese dialect. He kept moving as quietly as he could. He heard a voice giving orders directly in front of him. He readied his rifle as he lowered himself to the ground. The person giving orders passed within a few feet of him. He started moving again as soon as his heart stopped pounding. His feet and legs felt like they were made of rubber. He started moving faster. He heard a VC yell that only one was dead and the other must be in the area. He stopped and looked at his compass. He was traveling at 180 degrees. Close enough. The underbrush was ripping at his clothes. He put the rifle on safe, just in case he tripped or caught the trigger on something. He started running. There was a deafening roar. He could barely see the light from the flames as the plane went up. He'd better just walk fast, he told himself, no telling what was underfoot, and he could easily break his leg.

He had moved steadily for about an hour when he stopped and sat down. His lungs were bursting. Listening for any unusual sounds and hearing nothing, but his heart pounding, he took out his canteen and took a small sip of water. Pouring a little into the palm of his hand, he rubbed it over his face. His temples were still pounding. His watch read 0200. It meant he only had about four hours to get to the pickup site. He forced himself to start moving again. Something made him stop. Noises were coming from his left rear. He started walking fast again. If he could only make it to the edge of the jungle he would have it made. He could call in the reaction forces if necessary. He moved faster and started feeling himself get weak again. Sitting down on what appeared to be a ridge, he took out one of his SF energy bars and ate it as slowly as possible. Otherwise he knew he would be sick. Sticking the paper in his pocket he started moving again. The packet of codes was starting to rub him raw next to his skin. He thought about putting it somewhere else, but decided against it. His watch read 0500 hours. He should be coming to the clearing soon. He was going on a 170 azimuth now, he shouldn't be far off.

He was moving as fast as he could and had been going for another thirty minutes when he noticed it getting light up ahead. He had reached the edge of the jungle. Cautiously he moved forward. Sure enough, there it was. He could see moonlight up above. He had made it.

He stayed on the edge of the jungle. The sky was starting to lighten. It would be light in another hour. He took his small radio out of the rucksack. There was no reason why he should not be able to make contact. Before turning it on he listened for voices . He was sure they were still following him. Hearing none, he turned on the radio and set the frequency. He made the initial call and was surprised to hear them answer immediately. He gave the code word for mission accomplished and the casualty. He was informed to turn on his beacon locator. He also informed them he was being pursued and the pickup could prove to be a bit sticky. He received a roger and out.

He must have dozed momentarily. He was startled by the sound of aircraft and choppers coming in. He turned on his radio and monitored his pickup ship. At the same time he heard small arms fire coming from the clearing about two hundred meters to his left. He informed the choppers they were receiving small arms and the location they were coming from. A group of five choppers set down almost directly in front of him and out came the members of the reaction force. He started moving to one of the choppers when he got the word over the radio to stay in place. But it was too late, fire was now coming from the right and he had been spotted. He was not able to get back to the hiding place. The fire was building up. The reaction force was now raking the tree line with MG fire. He got the word to make a run for it. He got up and started running. He had about 200 feet to go when his right knee exploded. He must have blacked out momentarily, for he was lying on the ground. His rifle was about five feet from him. Bullets were tearing at the ground all around him. He looked at his knee, his pants were soaked with a dark red stain. He pulled off his belt and secured it tightly around his thigh. There was no feeling in the leg below the knee. He tried crawling but the pain in the knee was excruciating. He was afraid he would lose consciousness. His radio was blaring. He felt something tear into his right arm. With his left arm he grabbed the radio and informed the chopper he was hit and unable to move. He got a roger, and was told that help was on the way. He laid back and caught a glimpse of Spooky, A C-47 "Gooney Bird" with three 20 mm Vulcan MG, each capable of firing 6000 rounds a minute. Spooky was hosing down the wooded area and the enemy fire subsided.

The reaction force started withdrawing and was getting picked up by the choppers that had brought them in. His pickup chopper moved up to him and two people jumped off with a stretcher. He was loaded aboard and they took off. He could see Spooky still hosing down the area and covering their withdrawal.

"You're going to be all right," one of the crew chiefs informed him.

Tom told them he needed a shot of morphine, which the crew chief administered immediately. He kept dozing off. When they reached the airstrip, Bert was waiting for him with a doctor who looked at his knee and arm. The doctor left the tourniquet in place and told the crew chiefs to load him on the waiting Agency plane.

Bert leaned over him as they took off and informed him that they were taking him to the hospital in Da Nang and that everything would be all right. Tom reached inside his shirt and pulled out the code package.

"Engles bought it. We got to the plane about ten minutes ahead of them. They must have seen us drop."

"I heard your radio transmission. Our Blackbird saw the explosion and reported the plane still burning this morning. Don't talk anymore, we'll go over everything tomorrow," said Bert, squeezing his shoulder.

He fell asleep and vaguely remembered being offloaded

and driven to the hospital. In the hospital a doctor cut off his clothing and put an IV into his arm. He was told they were putting him to sleep. He waved his hand, indicating that he understood.

He woke up and was feeling sick to his stomach. The only thing he had on was a sheet over his body. He looked around and saw Bert and a doctor standing at the foot of his bed.

"If you take some deep breaths it will clear your lungs," the doctor told him.

He did as he was told and started feeling a little better.

"How do you feel, Tom?" Bert asked.

"My leg really hurts, especially my foot."

The doctor looked at Bert and said, "I've got something here for your pain." He took a small syringe and tested it and stuck it into his arm. "We had to take your leg off Tom, there was no way we could save it. The bullet had just about severed your knee."

He didn't want to hear anymore. The pain was subsiding. He went back to sleep.

THE PIT

Coming out of the operating anesthesia was something Pete dreaded. He always felt sick to his stomach.

"Take deep breaths and you'll feel better," he heard a voice in the distance say. He was gagging and coughing. The IV was still in his arm; his whole body was racked with pain. His hip, where they had taken the donor bone graft from, felt like it was on fire. His hand was throbbing. He asked the voice he had heard for a pain shot.

"I'm sorry, but you have to be completely awake before you can get something. And you know you have to void also."

These fucking recovery room nurses were all alike, and he

told her so. He told her to get Doc Berg immediately.

"Now, now, don't get nasty again. You are one of the foulest individuals I have ever heard coming out of anesthesia."

He turned his head so he could see or get a look at her. She was an enlisted WAC nurse. He recognized her; she was screwing a Lieutenant in the next room to The Pit. Her husband was in the Navy, currently serving in Vietnam. He told her again to get Doctor Berg and again she refused. He felt himself going into a rage. He was strapped to the bed and unable to move. The pain was almost unbearable.

"Here is a urinal, try to go. Otherwise I can't help you." She lifted up the sheet which was the only thing he had on, and placed the metallic bottle between his legs.

"Can you do it yourself or do you want me to help you?"

He informed her he was capable of taking care of himself and for her to get the hell away from him.

"My, oh my, a real tiger."

He knew he had to urinate or he wouldn't get a pain shot. He felt his body relax and soon the warm liquid was going into the bottle. He informed the WAC that he was done and for her to get Doc Berg.

"I'm here, Pete," he heard the familiar voice behind him. Coming around the side of the bed, Doc Berg asked how it was going.

He told him it was the worst pain he had ever experienced; that his whole body was hurting.

"Give me the bottle and I'll get you something. Remember, we told you that the bone grafting would be the worse one."

While waiting for Doctor Berg to come back, he was on the verge of screaming out in pain to let the goddam world know how he was suffering. How the hell had he gotten mixed up in this fucking war, anyway? And for what? He was on the verge of tears. He knew he could not let himself cry. God, he hadn't cried in over twenty years. He had to think of something to get his mind off the pain. The WAC - that was it. That shit head WAC who was fucking everybody while her husband was in the war. He thought of all the things he would do to her if she was his wife. He would probably kill her slowly. He would beat her so she would never be able to sleep with another man again. He could see the pain on her face as he beat her and heard her screams and moans.

All of a sudden he realized it was not the WAC's screams he was hearing. He was back in Vietnam; it was the screams of the prisoners they had captured whose information they were trying to extract from them. His Montagnard mercenaries had been good. They had made the prisoners talk, but not until they had made special examples of a few of them. He could hear them screaming. It sounded great to hear their animalistic cries, the blood running down their bodies. He only wished they had cut all of them up like his interrogator had wanted to. Those slope bastards. If he ever got the chance again he would show no mercy.

Jesus, he was hurting. Where the hell was Berg? What was taking him so long? He was getting warm, but his feet were freezing. The only thing he had on was the lousy sheet. He was naked. Why hadn't they given him some pajamas? That bitch WAC had probably enjoyed seeing him naked. Some of them were like that. Oh God, he wished he had a VC in his sights. He remembered the two he had got the week before he was hit. They had come right at him, not seeing him until it was too late. He had carefully moved his selector switch to full automatic. They had been less than 15 feet from his position when he had emptied the entire magazine into both of them, quickly reloading. The thought made him feel better. Both had lost control of their bladders, a phenomenon which he had observed to almost all the ones they had killed. The pain wasn't so bad anymore. He knew the docs would fix him up so he could get back to Vietnam and even up the score. He must have moved, for his hip was on fire again. No, he hadn't moved, he was having muscle spasms in his upper thigh. Where the hell was Doc Berg? That rotten fucker was doing it on purpose. Taking his time. Maybe he was back in some closet fucking that WAC. It was common knowledge that the doctors were fucking anything that walked. He couldn't believe it; Berg, who appeared to be so straight. How could he lower himself to fucking an enlisted WAC? Oh Christ, what was the world coming to, anyway?

"Here we are," he heard Doc Berg say. "I added some extra stuff to the Demerol because I don't think Demerol alone will help much. This should take care of it."

He noticed that the WAC had the needle and was giving him the shot. He could feel his heart quickening a little as she stuck the needle into his arm. And then came the calming effect. He asked Berg if he could go back to The Pit.

"I have already called down. Someone will be here in a few minutes to pick you up. What's the matter, don't you like it here? You have a good looking nurse to take care of you."

"I don't think he likes me," he heard the nurse say.

He wanted to say something crude to her, but the shot had started working. So instead he apologized to her and told her he would buy her a beer when he got up again. She accepted his offer.

He felt himself drowsing off. God, it felt good. He didn't have a care in the world. He heard voices and felt his bed being moved. He didn't bother opening his eyes. He felt secure and knew they were taking him back to The Pit. He dozed off.

He opened his eyes and saw the green curtains around his bed. There was no motion anymore. His bed was still. Bjorkvik was putting on his orthopedic pajamas. Seeing his eyes open she had asked how he was doing. He had indicated he was feeling okay.

"I hear you were nasty again coming out of the operating room. And also gave the WAC in recovery a hard time. In fact, you were nasty to everyone. You have to start thinking pleasant things before you go under anesthesia, that way you won't be like that when you wake up."

He felt a smile forming on his lips. He told her he loved her and that he would meet her at Happy Hour Friday night at 6:00 PM sharp.

She had sat down on the chair next to his bed and took his hand. "I don't know about you, Captain Compton, you are still fighting the war. You have to let go of it or it can hurt you permanently."

He was half in a daze, but could hear her words. She was a beautiful girl.

"You are a strange man. I have a feeling there are two of you. There is the quiet you and there is the violent you. You are going to have to forget and forgive, otherwise you will destroy yourself and alienate those who love you."

What the hell was she talking about? He really didn't care; he felt good - he was drifting into space.

Bjorkvik was not sure he had heard or understood what she was trying to tell him. In fact, she would not had said what she had, had she been sure he was awake. She had wanted to talk to him ever since Thanksgiving when they had made love and spent the weekend together. He had really frightened her. When they had made love she had the feeling that he was trying to kill her. Later his nightmare and talking in his sleep had kept her awake most of the night. His descriptive details of the torturing of prisoners and his obvious enjoyment in making them talk scared her. From what she had heard, he hadn't exactly been pining after her, but had participated in a wild party, a fact which really bothered her more than she cared to admit. She decided that she would invite him over for a nice dinner as soon as he was mobile again.

It had been a quiet weekend. Everyone who had had surgery was bedridden and were receiving pain medications. By Sunday afternoon Pete was feeling pretty good. He could make it to the bathroom even though the pain was almost unbearable when he moved. However he had never mastered the art of using the bedpan, so there was little choice. He still had another day of pain medication coming. Lt Bjorkvik came around about every four hours, and offered it if needed. The medication consisted of a shot of Demerol, which caused one to go into never-never land, and sort of float away mentally. No wonder people got hooked on it. It relieved not only the pain, but all of one's cares and anxieties also.

It was time for another shot, and Bjorkvik came around. Some of the members who had surgery had been taken off the Demerol shots already and were given Darvon pills instead. The Darvon was a super aspirin and helped alleviate the milder pains.

"Hey Bjorkvik, I really need a shot." It was Tom, his leg had given him trouble all weekend. However the doctor had only ordered medication through Sunday morning. "My leg is really killing me."

"You know I have to have the doctor's permission, Cpt Connor. I can't just authorize it on my own. I'll try and get the doctor on call to authorize it. The regular doctors don't make rounds on Sundays."

"Okay, but hurry, all right?" Tom looked miserable.

Bjorkvik left immediately and was back in two minutes. "The doctor is tied up in Emergency. There was a car accident and four people are seriously hurt."

Pete had motioned for her to come over to his bed. He told

her to give Tom his shot. No one would know the difference. Besides, he was feeling good and didn't need it.

"Do you want me to get kicked out of the Army?" she whispered, looking at him questioningly.

"If anyone finds out, Colonel Hayden will have my skin." He had assured her that the others would not know, and it was between her, Tom, and himself.

"This is going to cost you, Pete," she said, still whispering, but with a smile on her face, "so you better get well fast."

He smiled and assured her would think of some form of repayment.

She had taken the syringe of Demerol meant for him and gone over to Tom's bed. Leaning over she whispered something to Tom, who immediately rolled up his sleeve so she could give him the pain killing shot. Afterwards, Tom looked over at Pete and held up his hand, giving him a sign of thanks.

Pete noticed there were several visitors down by the nurses' station. Tracy, Sandusky's girl of late, came into The Pit. "Hi guys, how is everyone feeling? Fine, I hope."

She walked over to Sandusky's bed. He was asleep. He'd been suffering from a bad hangover all morning. She pulled the curtain around the bed and disappeared inside. There was a squeaking of the bed, some muffled voices, and then quiet.

An elderly couple walked in with Bjorkvik. Jim, upon seeing them, yelled out. "Hi folks, great to see you! Hey guys, I want you to meet my folks. They flew up here from Memphis."

Introductions were made, with the exception of Sandusky.

It was obvious that Jim's parents were sheltered southern people, who had not wandered far from home before. There was a lot of small talk about what they had seen flying up. Jim had informed them that everyone in the room had just had surgery, and were still a little under the weather. His mother looked around the room and seemed almost apologetic for having come to visit her son.

Bjorkvik had taken a seat by Pete's bed and was making small talk. "I bought a couple of nice steaks yesterday. You think you'll feel up to a nice dinner Thursday night? I'm off on Friday and Saturday."

He had informed her that one time she had invited him over for something to eat, namely scrambled eggs, and he hadn't gotten much in the way of food.

"Didn't you like the main course?" she said mockingly. "I think we'd better do a hormone count on you. No, I take that back, your hormones are fine. You're just a little confused; I fed you well that night, in fact...." She didn't finish the sentence.

Everyone in The Pit was looking towards Sandusky's bed. Two shoes had fallen to the floor with a bang, barely visible under the curtain. They were not Sandusky's, that was obvious. From behind the curtains came moans, and the bed was obviously moving about.

"Oh my God," Bjorkvik whispered. "Please say it isn't so."

Louder groans were now emanating from behind the curtain.

"Is there something we can do for that poor boy?" Jim's mother asked. "Should I go over and comfort him?"

A look of sheer terror appeared on Bjorkvik's face.

"Ma'am, there isn't much you can do to help him," said John. "He has these spells and I'm sure it won't last much longer."

The noises were now becoming quite obvious to everyone in The Pit except for Jim's parents.

"That-a-way, Sandusky, drive it in there, you son of a gun." It was Tom. The shot had really hit him. Bjorkvik rushed over to his bed and calmed him down. She told him to be quiet or he wouldn't get any more pain shots.

"I do want to help him," said Mrs. Brooks again, as the

noises from Sandusky's bed continued; she started moving toward the bed.

"No, mom, don't go near the bed, please," Jim said, looking white as a sheet.

"Mrs. Brooks, I'll take care of it," Bjorkvik said, intercepting her half way across the room. "I can assure you it's almost over," Bjorkvik said, looking at her watch with concern, and leading Mrs. Brooks back to Jim's bed.

"You know," said Mr. Brooks, "I could almost swear there are two people behind those curtains."

"No sir, I can assure you Mr. Sandusky is quite alone." With that, Bjorkvik moved toward Sandusky's bed. A look of total desperation appeared on her face. A loud cry came from behind the curtains, and then silence. Bjorkvik didn't know what to do.

"Why don't you see if he needs some help," said Childres. Bjorkvik glared at him in utter disbelief. "I think you'd better," Childres said again. "It could get worse."

Bjorkvik opened the curtains quickly and disappeared behind them. There were some muffled voices, and Bjorkvik reappeared, her face beet red.

"Everything is all right. Mr. Sandusky is fine," she said. She moved over to the chair by Pete's bed again, and sat down.

Jim hobbled out of bed. "Well, I think we'll go down to the lounge for a while." He said, indicating for his parents to follow him.

"We sure enjoyed meeting you all," said Mrs. Brooks. "Give our regards to that poor Mr. Sandusky. I hope he gets well real soon." As soon as they had left The Pit, Bjorkvik put her head in her arms, leaning on Pete's bed.

"I can't believe it, I can't believe it. Thank God I only have thirty minutes left on this shift," she whispered.

He took a bottle of scotch out of his nightstand and poured

some into his water glass. He indicated for her to take a sip.

"I can't, but I'll be back as soon as Mrs. Foster comes on. I see she's already here. Not one word about this. I'll personally deal with Mr. Sandusky." She walked out of The Pit.

Sandusky staggered out from behind the curtains. His appearance brought silence to The Pit. He looked around, seeing only familiar faces and said, "What the hell is all the fuss about anyway? The Lieutenant busted into my private area here, and well...." He walked into the bathroom. The curtains around his bed opened. Tracy was sitting on his bed nonchalantly smoking a cigarette. She looked down at her feet and realized that she didn't have any shoes on. "Now where could they have gone?" she said, speaking to no one in particular. "I know I had them on when I came in here." Finding the shoes by the foot of the bed, she forced her feet into them. "Well, I guess I'd better leave you boys, so you can get some rest. Tell Freddie I'll see him at the O club." Having said that she departed The Pit.

No one said anything. Tom was sacked out and snoring.

"I don't want to seem like a prude, but what just happened here could have had some dire consequences," Childres said, getting up from his bed and hobbling over to The Pit table. He sat down on a chair and propped his bad leg up on another chair. "I think we'd better establish some firm ground rules, otherwise there will be a Pit no more."

"I agree," said John. "What just happened could have ended Bjorkvik's career in the Army, not to mention the embarrassment to Jim's parents. You know, when his mother walked toward that bed, I prayed for the first time in fifteen years. The time has come to issue Sandusky an ultimatum. Either he cleans up his act, or we see the doc about getting him out of here. Childres, why don't you have a heart to heart talk with him, in some private place? Give him one of your fatherly lectures. I know he thinks a lot of you," John said, almost pleadingly.

"Do we all agree on this before I have my chat with him?"

Everyone concurred. Sandusky walked out of the bathroom, going straight to his bed. "Hey, where did she go? That bitch, she left."

"Take it easy, Fred," said Childres. "She said she'd meet you later at the club."

Sandusky didn't answer, but sat on his bed staring at the floor. "Okay, I heard your conversation in here while I was in the head. Let me tell you guys something. There isn't a person in here who's a fucking virgin lily."

"Fucking virgin! Where?" It was Tom who had woken up at the sound of Sandusky's loud voice.

No one paid any attention to him, except Bjorkvik, who happened to walk into The Pit at that moment. Walking over to Tom's bed, she put her hand on his forehead. "How are you feeling, Cpt Connor? How is your leg, better I hope?" She had her coat on and was ready to go home.

"As I was saying," Sandusky went on, "don't give me that high and mighty attitude, any of you. How was I to know we had visitors?"

"Listen, Mr. Sandusky, there isn't a person in this room who's against having fun. However, Jim is a member of The Pit, and has as much right as anyone, and that includes bringing his parents in here to visit him." Bjorkvik was mad and getting madder with each word. He had never seen her this way. Her blue eyes were flashing. The tip of her nose was white. "We don't have to be embarrassed by some stupid inconsiderate person. I'm going to leave it up to you men to do what is right. But I'll tell you this. This better not happen again or I'll press charges against the guilty individual."

No one said a word. Sandusky looked around the room, not saying anything. Bjorkvik walked out of The Pit.

Before anyone could say anything, Mrs. Foster walked

in pushing the medication cart. "Why's everyone looking so glum?" she said, with a twinkle in her eye. "I haven't seen this place so quiet in two years working here. What's the matter, Mr. Sandusky? Someone take the starch out of you? Well, you'll get over it. I do have an announcement for you though. I'll be taking a two week vacation starting Thursday. Mrs. Blake over in Ward 2 will be over here at night. John, you know her. She gets a little excited at times."

She was passing out the medications as she was talking. When she got to Pete's bed she held up the syringe with Demerol. He told her he would try to get along without it, and if there was any chance of Tom getting it instead, since he was in pain.

"Lt Bjorkvik has made arrangements for him with the duty doctor, so he will get a shot. I'll just keep this for you in case you want it later. How come Lt Bjorkvik was so upset when she left here tonight? I've never seen her like that," she whispered. "You two have a fight?" She moved off with a sly smile on her face.

When she got over to Sandusky's bed she looked at him closely. "You know, you don't look so good. I think you'd better go up to the club and have a drink."

Sandusky looked at her, got his clothes and disappeared into the bathroom to change.

"My, oh my, someone is not in a very good mood, is he?" She didn't wait for a reply, but gave George his medication and ambled out of The Pit pushing her cart.

Tom was having a problem after his last surgery on his leg. He had gone a week without having a bowel movement. He finally told Bjorkvik about it, and she and a corpsman closed the curtains and administered a pill rectally. About an hour went by and nothing happened. The doctor was not around so Bjorkvik notified her chief nurse, LTC Hayden; within five minutes LTC Hayden burst through the swinging doors into the "Pit."

"Are you telling me, with all your training, you can't get a patient to have a bowel movement?" Bjorkvik told her what she had done without any results.

All the other "Pit" members were watching the drama unfold.

LTC Hayden left the "Pit" and returned a few minutes later with a red rubber bag with a long tube leading from it. Her starch white uniform made a swishing noise as she walked over to Tom's bed. She appeared agitated that she had been summoned to perform such a trivial task. She informed Bjorkvik and the corpsman that there was more than one way to get this job done.

"Get the bedpan," LTC Hayden yelled at the corpsman. She also instructed him to pour a portion of a small brown bottle she handed him into the red rubber bag to which she had already added some warm water. She then instructed the corpsman to hold the rubber bag up above Tom and to follow her behind the closed curtains. Bjorkvik remained outside the curtains.

The "Pit" members could hear LTC Hayden tell Tom to turn over on his side. They assumed she was inserting the tube from the red rubber bag into his rectum.

"Let's give him all the liquid in the bag," LTC Hayden instructed the corpsman. "And hold the bedpan ready."

What happened next was difficult to say. There was a sound of gas and feces exploding out, hitting the green curtains around Tom's bed and a metal bedpan falling on the floor and a female scream mixed with adjectives normally used by a unit's first sergeant.

"Get the bedpan," LTC Hayden screamed at the corpsman, who evidently had had enough because he appeared from behind the curtains covered in several shades of brown feces, dragging the rubber bag and tube with him heading for the showers, which could be heard being turned on.

LTC Hayden appeared covered from head to her shoes in feces. "Get a cleanup crew down here and get the patient cleaned up," she yelled at Bjorkvik and departed at a rather fast pace. The members of the "Pit" roared. Sandusky walked into the shower section with a robe and to see what he could do to help the corpsman. Bjorkvik departed for the nurse's station to phone for a cleanup crew, which appeared within five minutes. They removed the green curtain, stripped the bed and cleaned the floor. Tom was cleaned and a new bed was brought in, and the entire area was disinfected.

Tom was lying on his bed and announced to the "Pit" members that he felt better now. Bjorkvik appeared and went over to Tom to make sure he was all right. She then addressed the "Pit" members.

"No jokes from anyone about this. You all know LTC Hayden, so let's not antagonize her. Enough said. No need to say anything. The entire orthopedic ward already knows." However stern Bjorkvik tried to be, she left the "Pit" with a slight smile. Immediately upon her departure, the jokes started, but Tom took it good naturedly.

Pat walked into the "Pit" and waved at everyone and proceeded over to Tom's bed. "You look really good today," she said as she gave Tom a kiss. Tom was lying on top of his bed in a pair of blue hospital pajamas. "If I didn't know better, I'd say you have lost some weight," she said as she ran her hand over his chest and stomach.

The rest of the "Pit" members burst out laughing. "What's going on?" she said. "I'm sorry, Pat," said Childres, trying to be stern. "We are not allowed to talk about it. You will have to ask Bjorkvik." Bjorkvik walked in with her coat on. "Are you ready, Pat?" "Yes, besides the commissary, I also need to stop by the PX. Does anyone here need anything?"

"Yes, could you get me something for my stomach, Pat? I've been a little constipated lately," Sandusky said with a grimace on his face.

"Sure, Tom is having problems also. Maybe you guys are not drinking enough."

"Never mind, Pat," Bjorkvik said taking her by the arm and leading her out of the "Pit."

"You know," said John, "Maybe we aren't drinking enough. Who has a bottle in his bed stand?"

GEORGE'S STORY

George had grown up in a small town in Alabama. He was a quiet unassuming young man. During his first year in high school he had made the varsity football squad, a feat which would have turned anyone else's head, but not young George. He did everything well in school and early predictions had him pegged as a sure scholarship candidate to the University.

George learned that along with his fame as a halfback also came a certain admiration from the young ladies, not only those in the high school, but those already out of school as well. Unlike his contemporaries, George did not have his first experience with women in the local road house at the edge of town.

Instead, a widow in her early forties, whose husband had been a state legislator, befriended George. At first she had hired him to do odd jobs after school, but after a while George was spending more time just talking and sampling her latest cake or batch of cookies, than actually working.

One day she had asked him what he thought of her. He

had told her he thought she was a very nice lady.

"Are you saying that just because I pay you good wages for doing next to nothing, or do you think I'm really nice?"

"No ma'am, I think you are a fine lady, Mrs. Howes. In fact you are extremely attractive."

"I enjoy hearing that, George, no one tells me that anymore, and by-the-way, call me Mary Lou; Mrs. Howes sounds so formal. It's very lonesome for a woman my age not to have a man around. George, I want to ask you something very personal. Now, you don't have to answer if you don't want to, but George, have you ever been with a woman? I don't mean dating some of the young high school girls, I mean really been with a woman?"

"I'm not sure I understand," George said in a quiet voice. He did understand, all right. This had been coming for some time. Mrs. Howes had been somewhat less than subtle in her interest in him.

"George, if I can be perfectly frank with you, what I mean is, have you ever gone to bed with a woman?"

George lowered his eyes and shook his head. "No ma'am," he said in a low voice.

"George, I'm much older than you. What I mean is, I'm a few years your senior, but that doesn't make any difference to me, so it shouldn't to you. The women out at the roadhouse are older than I am."

"Yes ma'am."

"Call me Mary Lou, George."

"Yes, Mary Lou."

"George, does that mean you would like to go to bed with me?"

"Yes ma'am, I mean Mary Lou."

Mrs. Howes took George by the hand and led him upstairs to her bedroom. She removed her clothes and helped George remove his.

"You are a fine young man, George," she said, as George stood naked before her. Pulling back the covers of the bed and laying down she commanded, "Come here."

"Yes ma'am," George said in a trembling voice.

"Call me Mary Lou, George."

George started spending more time at Mrs. Howes' house. Instead of going over only after school, he was now spending a good portion of Saturdays there also. The football coach was starting to notice the change in George. He was not paying as much attention to the plays and it seemed his heart was not in the game.

At the end of the spring practice in his third year, the coach pulled George aside and told him he had been cut from the squad.

"I've talked to you before, George. You have tremendous potential, but I think you've been sidetracked. Is it the widow Howes? The boys tell me you practically live over there."

George didn't answer. He walked into the locker room, showered and changed.

"How come so quiet today? Your mind seems a thousand miles away. Don't you enjoy our afternoons anymore?"

George got out of bed and walked into the bathroom. When he came back out Mrs. Howes was getting dressed.

"I won't be coming here anymore, Mrs. Howes."

"Oh my, it's Mrs. Howes now. You haven't called me that in over a year. Have you been back-seating it with some of the young girls in the car I practically bought for you?"

"No, it's not that."

"Come on, George, we've been honest with each other. Let's not spoil what we have by some impetuous act."

"I'm going into the Army."

The words stunned her. She sat back down on the bed. Her

unsnapped bra hanging down her front.

"The Army! Why, you haven't finished High School yet. You were going to the University. What's happened? Am I scaring you, George? I'm getting too possessive, is that it? That is it, isn't it?"

"No, I have just decided to quit school and get the service over with."

Neither one spoke as they both finished dressing. George walked out the door without saying another word.

His parents had to sign for him because of his age. They had protested initially, but had consented in the end. George had enjoyed basic training and had scored high on his aptitude tests. Through a special program after basic he had received his High School Diploma. His First Sergeant had asked him one day if he was interested in the Warrant Officer Flight program. He had not thought about it, but decided to try it.

In addition to learning how to fly, there had also been much harassment meted out by the senior Warrant Officer candidates. There had been days when he was actually too tired from running and doing pushups to fly the helicopter. After completing the basics at Fort Wolters, Texas, he along with the other WOs had been sent to Fort Rucker, Alabama for the second stage of their training. At Ft. Rucker there was no harassment, only long hours of flying and classroom work. On several weekends he had gone home but had not stopped by the widow Howes' place.

Upon graduation from flight school, he had been assigned to the 1st Infantry Division of Fort Riley, Kansas, which was in the process of deploying to Vietnam.

George had been in Vietnam less than a month. One day as he was flying co-pilot and going in to pick up a wounded platoon leader near the Michelin rubber plantation, the chopper took several rounds through the floor. One of the rounds went through George's foot and shattered his leg bone in several places. He slumped over, grabbing his bloody leg, The pilot saw and immediately turned the chopper back and headed for the 1st Division Hospital.

The entire ordeal had been undramatic. Because of the shattered bone, George had been evacuated back to the States.

THE PIT

Mrs. Blake was in her fifties, a widow with a son at West Point. Her whole life was centered around her son. Any chance she had, she would tell anyone who would listen about her cadet son. She was about 5'2" tall, slim to the point of being skinny, with a pale complexion. Her wire-rimmed glasses hung low on her nose. The slightest thing would set her off. During the night she would come around with her flashlight, shining it directly into the patient's face and ultimately touching him to determine if he was still alive. Between the light and her "Death Touch", as it was called by the members of The Pit, the Patients usually woke up with a bright light shining in his face. It was usually a startling awakening and very irritating. She would immediately tell the patient, when she saw his eyes open, to go back to sleep. After the fourth night of this, Tom was getting extremely agitated.

"I have had a hard enough time going to sleep, the way my leg is acting up, but then to get woken up by that nut only to be told to go to sleep is too much."

"You know, I was awake the other night," said John, "and she came in here at least six times checking on us in less than two hours. Foster doesn't come in unless someone is in bad shape."

"Why don't we set her up? I'll bet she has heard stories about all the wild things going on in here, and is trying to catch us. Hey, Sandusky, didn't you say Tracy worked in a women's clothing store?"

"Yeah, a real exclusive one. Why?"

"Well, why don't you call her up and get a manikin, female type, with stockings and a pair of high heeled shoes on?"

"What the hell you want that for?" Sandusky said with a puzzled look on his face.

"Never mind, just tell her we want to borrow it. She can return it tomorrow."

Sandusky got up and walked down to the nurses' station to make his call.

"We put the manikin in Jim's bed," said Tom. Jim was about to protest but was cut off. "With her legs sticking out of the covers, and with Mrs. Blake's eyesight, and in the dark, she'll think it's the real thing."

"She'll flip," said John. "But we'd better have a plan for getting rid of the manikin. Maybe stick it in the latrine, or in one of the lockers."

Sandusky came back from his call. "She thinks we're crazy or mentally deranged, but she's bringing one over tonight, with all the trimmings. It will be a redhead, by the way."

True to her word, Tracy arrived at 6:00 PM. "I need some help with your new girl, guys. I had a hard time explaining to my boss why I was borrowing a female manikin, but he was sweet about it. Even helped put it in my car."

"Okay, let's get it in here. Put it in the shower," said Tom.

George and Sandusky went out and brought it in.

"Hey, she's not bad looking. I think I'll give her a try," quipped Sandusky, after having placed it in the latrine.

"Listen, you can't handle what you've got," said Tracy, pulling Sandusky by the arm. "Come on, you owe me a drink. Bye, guys, have a good time." She and Sandusky departed The Pit.

By the time Mrs. Blake came around with the night's

medication, everyone was in on the plan. No one spoke as she passed out the medication and the ration of beer and whiskey.

"I really think it's wrong to give you boys whiskey and beer. If I had anything to say about it, you wouldn't get a thing. Some of you aren't sick anymore. From what I hear, all you people do here is get into mischief."

"Mrs. Blake, if I was a little older, I sure would like to give you a whirl," John said with a straight face. "You are an extremely attractive woman. I'll be you have boyfriends all over the place."

"Well, I had my share….never mind, Mr. Snyder. I don't like what you're driving at. You keep your thoughts to yourself. It's lights out." She switched off the main light, and left The Pit.

"Okay, let's get it, Jim. Childres, give me a hand," John directed.

The manikin was placed in alongside Jim. The feet and part of the legs were visible. The red hair was the only thing showing above the covers. In the semi-dark room it looked like the real thing. The high heeled shoes were placed on the floor at the foot of the bed.

"Hey, she's pretty nice and cooperative," whispered Jim, "but she hasn't got a….."

"Shut up or I'll tell Linda you're cheating on her," said Childres. "George, put a chair in front of the doors so it's a little harder for Mrs. Blake to get in here. That should immediately arouse her suspicions.

An hour went by, and some of The Pit members had dozed off. It was almost 11:30 when someone whispered, "She's coming."

The door banged against the chair.

"What is this?" Mrs. Blake said in an irritated voice, as she pushed the chair to the side.

She stood by the door, flashing her light around the room.

A gasp emanated from her throat as she flashed the light at Jim's bed. She took a few steps toward his bed then halted again, shining her light over the bed. The light hit the long red hair on the pillow next to his head, and picked up the exposed legs as she illuminated the bed. She started walking backwards to the door.

"Now all of you stay right here," she yelled, "Not one of you make a move."

She turned on the overhead lights. Jim quickly flipped the covers over the exposed legs.

"I know what you have there, Mr. Brooks, don't try to hide her. You get out of the bed, you hear me?"

"Yes, Mrs. Blake," Jim said sheepishly.

"Not you, her. Get out! Get out!" Mrs. Blake was yelling at the top of her voice. "Oh, I'll get the OD. He'll get you out, you…you…you hussy!" Mrs. Blake stalked out.

"Hey, get your friend in the locker, Jim," Childres whispered.

George came over and together they put the manikin and her shoes in a narrow metal wall locker and snapped the lock.

"Did you see the look on her face?" Tom was in hysterics. Everyone was laughing.

"Quiet, here they come." Sandusky had been standing by the door.

In walked Dr. Weber, the OD, NCO, and Mrs. Blake.

"She's over there, Dr. Weber." Mrs. Blake was pointing to John's bed, not moving from the door.

"I have had this room under observation so no one has left."

Dr. Weber and the NCO walked over to Jim's bed and pulled the covers back.

"Can I help you?" Jim said in a sleepy voice.

Dr. Weber looked around the room and behind the open bed curtains.

"I know she is in here, I saw her myself," Mrs. Blake protested when no one was found.

Dr. Weber told the NCO to check the latrine.

"Nothing in here, Doctor," said the NCO coming out of the latrine.

Dr. Weber looked around once more and departed with the NCO. Mrs. Blake followed them out and down the hallway.

"I tell you she was in there, Doctor. I saw her. They've hidden her." Mrs. Blake's high pitched voice could be heard throughout the ward. Lights were going on in the other rooms, and patients were sticking their heads out into the hallway wanting to know what was going on.

"I think this calls for a little celebration," said John. "I have to admit this little farce ranks with some of the best SF operations I've ever been involved with."

Tom produced a bottle and Jim poured a portion into everyone's glass.

"Well, here's to a good night's sleep. I don't think Mrs. Blake will be back tonight." Having said this, Tom drained his glass and laid down. Each one did the same.

"I have a premonition we will hear about this in the morning," said George. No one spoke. It was quiet in the "Pit" at night for the next week. Mrs. Blake never checked again, at least not to anyone's knowledge.

It was 11:30 AM and The Pit members were watching "Jeopardy" on TV. John came wheeling into The Pit in his wheelchair. As usual, the Wall Street Journal was laying across his lap.

We're getting a visitor, troops. Well, not exactly, he's a columnist from a newspaper, works for Drew Pearson. His name is Jack Anderson.

"I've read some of his stuff," said Childres. "He's what is known in journalistic circles as a muckraker. In fact, he's understudying Drew Pearson, the master."

"That's as good and as generous an introduction as I've ever had." No one had noticed a dark haired man in civilian clothes standing in the doorway. "I'm Jack Anderson, and believe me, I have enough information about this room, commonly referred to as The Pit, they tell me, to keep me writing for a month. But that's not my purpose here. May I sit down?"

Taking a seat by The Pit table he extracted a long narrow notebook from his pocket. "Let me be quite frank with you. I know all your names, and the most popular drink in this room is Wild Turkey, a bottle of which will be here within thirty minutes. Don't get me wrong, it's not a bribe, it's a present of appreciation."

"You've really done your homework. Are you always this thorough?" said Childres as he walked over and turned off the TV.

"Well, I have to be, otherwise there are all sorts of lawsuits and un-pleasantries. I came over here last week to visit an old friend who is dying of cancer, and I couldn't help but notice the decrepit condition this hospital is in. I'm referring to the physical structure, not the staff. Your doctors here are the best in the country."

"You know, it is an old hospital," said Childres, sounding like he was trying to defend it.

"I know that. However, is that any reason for not painting and proper cleaning? You guys have a pretty nice room, even though the ceiling is coming down, and your floor is peeling. But have you ever been in the back where some of the EM are living?"

"You may not realize it, but this hospital is getting crowded as hell. We are really taking it on the chops over there. The I Drang Valley operation landed over 200 new patients here."

He was right. They had talked about it many times. They

had all visited friends in the other wards where the EM were. Things were tight.

"My feeling is that a wounded GI returning from Nam should live under the best possible hospital conditions. I have talked to the comptroller here, and believe me, they have been more than candid with me. I have seen their cancelled requests for funds to spruce this place up. My purpose here is to tell it like it is, and maybe jar some money out of our fat congress and help this place."

He had asked them questions about maintenance teams, when they had seen one last, how long they had been there, if they had noticed the peeling paint in the hallways outside the ward, and so on. They had filled him in with everything they knew.

There was a knock on the double doors. Another man carrying a paper bag entered.

"Hi Stu, I'm almost done. By the way, this is Stu, my partner." Everyone signaled a hi to him. Stu removed two bottles from his bag.

"I knew about the bourbon, but I also found out that scotch was a close second, so this one is from me." Stu held up the bottle smiling. Everyone chimed in their thanks, and offered to toast a few.

"No thanks," said Anderson, "we've got to go." He got up and put his notebook back in his pocket, and went around shaking everyone's hand, thanking them.

"Oh, by the way," he said with a smile, "If you guys ever need another manikin, let me know. I know someone who would be happy to contribute one of those life size rubber dolls. They are more realistic looking." He waved his hand and left with Stu trailing behind him.

"My God, how the hell did he find out about that?" Tom said with a worried look on his face.

"Hell, the whole staff knew the next morning. It was the topic of conversation at Colonel Grange's staff meeting. Col Grange's deputy, LTC Baker, was briefed by the OD on the whole incident."

"Who told you, Sandusky?" Childres asked.

"I got it from one of the nurses."

"Why the hell didn't you tell us," yelled Tom.

"Well, I didn't want to worry you guys, but according to my friend, they all got a good laugh from it."

True to his word, Anderson's story on the hospital appeared in the Drew Pearson column the next week. It was a scathing expose on the deplorable conditions the wounded fighting men had to endure in one of the most prominent hospitals in the United States. He went on to compare the luxury suites for the VIPs and the squalor of the back wards. He did defend the effort to secure sufficient funds to fix the place up. He placed the blame on the Medical Command, the Surgeon General, and the Department of the Army.

His paper would use all available resources to see that this deplorable condition was remedied at the earliest opportunity. It took exactly one day for the congressional investigators to reach the hospital. They were followed by maintenance people and paint contractors. The priority went to the back wards where the enlisted men were living. It was a 24 hour around the clock effort. The hallways and areas where patients were not sleeping were fixed up at night.

It was amazing what a little paint and cleaning could do to brighten the place up. New ceilings and floors were installed; broken toilets and urinals replaced. After a month the place was hard to recognize. Even the "Pit" had been refurbished.

"Can you believe this is the same hospital? I never thought this could happen. At least not this fast. I think we should send Anderson a note of thanks. What do you guys think?"

said Childres.

All agreed and Childres was chosen to send the appropriate words.

"Hi guys." It was Pat and she was carrying a large manila envelope under her arm. She went over and kissed Tom on the cheek. "I have something for all of you," she said, holding up the large envelope. She reached into the envelope and withdrew a glossy sign, the top of which was a coiled snake in vivid colors and underneath was the painted the word PIT in large letters.

"Hey, that's beautiful, hon," said Tom.

"Yah, hon, it's great. Come here and I'll show you my appreciation," said John jokingly.

"I don't want to see your appreciation. I hear it's ugly. Anyway I saw it the other night when I brought Tom back. You ought to be more careful, John, about those pajamas of yours, especially sleeping without covers," said Pat, hitting John on top of his head.

John rolled on his bed in mock pain. "What can I say after a statement like that?"

"Don't say anything, let's get back to the sign," said Childres. "I think we should have an appropriate ceremony."

"I agree, and the sign should be hung directly outside and above the doors," Jim said, examining the sign. "You know, this is pretty good work. Who did it, Pat?"

"Tom's aunt, who lives in Bar Harbour, Maine, had it done by a local artist. I had the protective glaze put on at a picture store downtown."

"Let's just hang it up and see what happens," said George. "They may not let us keep it."

"I agree with George. Let's just hang it up and see if anyone notices it. Get a chair, George. I have some long tacks here that should hold it," said John.

They all agreed. Sandusky got a chair and proceeded to

hang the sign directly over the entrance leading into The Pit. Everyone commented on how good it looked.

"Every mother fucking room in this hospital will have a sign when they see this one."

"What was that second word you used, Sandusky? You know, they have English classes right here in the hospital two nights a week for those with a limited vocabulary," said Bjorkvik, joining them outside the room and admiring the sign.

"Well, I guess the Pit is now officially the "Snake Pit", said Bjorkvik.

She went in and came over to Pete's bed. "Do you feel like going out and eating some fresh boiled shrimp tonight? I heard of a nice little old-fashioned combination fish store and restaurant only about three blocks from here."

He asked her if she was treating. She had held up her little finger, saying "This is the ladylike way for you know what."

He informed her about the English classes held twice a week for those who had….. He had not finished. She took his water glass which was full and poured it down the front of his pajamas, soaking his front and the spot on the bed where he was lying.

She put her hands on her hips and said, "Well, what is it going to be, yes or no?"

He quickly informed her that he would take her out if she could get him an overnight.

"Have you got a place to stay tonight?" she said mockingly, "Or should I plan on fixing up the couch?"

He looked at her with a serious expression, and informed her that he had a date later that night with Tracy. She had promised to show him a new trick. He was not prepared for what happened next. Bjorkvik rolled up both the feet and the head of his bed at the same time, until the two ends were sticking straight up. He was caught in the middle and unable to move. His knees were almost touching his face. He felt the strain on his new stitches.

He saw Bjorkvik peering over the top where his feet were. He faked a faint, closing his eyes and slightly opening his mouth. She spoke to him several times. He didn't answer.

"Hey, are you okay, Pete?" She was starting to get concerned. "Answer me. Do you hear me? I know you're all right, you can't fool me." She sounded unsure. She closed the curtains around the bed and rolled the head of the bed down, with the foot portion slightly elevated. She was standing by his head putting her hand on his forehead.

"Pete, I'm sorry. Are you all right?" she whispered, with a sound of despair in her voice.

He slowly moved his hand down alongside of the bed. She was wiping his face with a wet cloth, talking to him. He moved his hand slowly up her leg under her uniform, not touching her legs until he had reached the desired spot between her legs. He finally placed his hand against her underpants feeling the silky material. She gasped out loud.

"Hey, is everything okay in there?" It was Pat.

"Yes, everything is under control," said Bjorkvik. "You bastard," she whispered, "I'll pay you back for this."

He kept his eyes closed, not moving his hand. She bent over and kissed his forehead. He removed his hand, and told her he loved her. He opened his eyes and saw she had tears welling up in her eyes. Not speaking, she took his hand in hers and squeezed it.

"Shall I ask Pat and Tom to join us for shrimps tonight?" He indicated yes.

"I'll pick you up later then, and I won't bother fixing up the couch for you. I have a new trick I want to show you." He smiled, not saying anything.

She opened the curtains and walked over to Tom and Pat.

They were both sitting on Tom's bed.

She had asked them about going out. He could not hear her exact words, but saw Tom looking over to him, giving him the okay sign. Tom was asking Bjorkvik something, pointing over to him. Pat had hit Tom on the shoulder, saying so he could hear, "That's none of our business, mister, keep your nose out."

Bjorkvik had walked away, checking on the other patients. He knew it was no longer a secret in the "Snake Pit", but he was still confused about this feelings toward her. That he loved her there was no doubt. But the future was so uncertain. There were just so many ifs.

The shrimp dinner had been great. It had been Tom's first night out of the hospital on his new leg. He had been going to physical therapy each day, practicing, and he was doing quite well.

"You still lurch a little, Tom," said Pat. "You sort of throw the prosthesis out in front of you."

"That will come with a little more practice, Pat; he is really doing great considering he has only had it two weeks." Bjorkvik's remarks seemed to put Tom at ease. He had appeared a little nervous going out tonight. The only strong drink they served was beer, and they were on their second pitcher when the shrimp arrived.

"This is fantastic. Dip them in the horseradish, it makes your eyes water," said Pat.

It was a pleasant meal. Tom and Pat were good company.

"What about you two? Are you going to get married or what?"

"Shut up, Tom, that's none of your business." Pat was irritated, as if she knew something.

"Listen, we've been out before and I don't even know Bjorkvik's first name. What is it?"

"It's Kristen, Tom. Most people call me Kris for short."

"Well, what's going on between you two? We know it's serious. We know that Jim and Linda are getting married. It's something you can't keep secret. Besides, you owe it to your fellow "Snake Pit" members to come clean."

"Tom, when we decide, you will be the first to know. Right, Pete?"

He had agreed. "You know," said Tom, "Pete here is sort of quiet. He doesn't say much. He's as bad as George."

"Not to change the subject, but the weather is starting to get warm. Wouldn't it be great to go sailing on the bay?" Bjorkvik sounded excited. "I used to go sailing on Lake Superior all the time during the spring and summer. It's really delightful."

"John knows how to sail. He went to school on the east coast, and was on the sailing team, or rather, the sailing club," Tom said. "Besides, I know a little."

Pete told them he thought they'd better go down and practice a little before they took along any passengers. It was agreed that the "Snake Pit" would conduct some shakedown cruises, and then would invite the girls. He had paid the check and they had said good night to Pat and Tom.

Driving to her apartment, they had both agreed that Tom and Pat were nice people. He had commented that Pat was a little overprotective about Tom.

"Well, he is still not home free, you know. They won't know for a while yet if the osteo has been arrested."

As they were walking down the hallway to her door, he had mentioned Tom's conversation regarding their situation. Once inside the apartment, he told her he loved her, but that things were so uncertain.

"I have seriously been thinking of volunteering for Vietnam. A lot of the other nurses are going, and I feel that that is where I belong. I have always been a joiner."

Her statement almost floored him. He felt himself getting weak. What the hell was the matter with her, he thought. He held her close. She put her arms around him and squeezed him tight.

"I don't know what I should do, Pete. You and I have been very frank with each other and I just felt I should tell you how I feel."

He had asked her for a drink. She had poured them both scotch on the rocks. They took a long sip and put their glasses on the table.

He turned to her and told her they were getting married. He would make the arrangements. John would be his best man.

"Are you serious? We can't just get married. It takes a lot of planning."

"Not this wedding," he had told her. He could tell she was happy.

"Aren't you going to propose or something? I always thought you were supposed to ask for my hand in marriage or something."

He told her to come into the bedroom. She had followed willingly, with her arms around him, kissing his neck.

CHILDRES' STORY

Dan Childres III was born an Army brat. The military was drilled into him from the earliest days. His grandfather and father had both been Generals, so from the beginning Dan Childres III knew for a fact that he would also be a General officer. He attended the Citadel Military Academy instead of West Point, not because he could not get an appointment there, but because his elders before him had been Citadel graduates.

Childres, as his friends called him, was an extremely serious young man. He planned his life during his last year at the Academy to include at what stage in his life he would get married. This was determined by rank rather than age or falling for the right girl. Marriage would come when he attained the rank of Lieutenant Colonel. At that stage, he determined, he would not be moving around too much, his career would have established a pattern.

Childres was commissioned in the Field Artillery, like his father. He attended the artillery schools and his first assignment was V Corps Artillery Headquarters in Frankfurt Germany.

Childres soon established a reputation as a perfectionist and a highly capable young officer. Unlike his fellow junior grade officers, he did not fraternize with the young ladies of Frankfurt. Instead he would spend his time taking correspondence courses for the advanced schools of the other service branches within the Army. After two years in Germany, he had completed five branch school courses with honors and received special recognition from the Artillery Branch.

While on winter maneuvers in Germany, an incident took place which had a profound effect on Childres and was to change his thinking about Army strategy. While acting as the duty officer in the Tactical Operations Center (TOC) of the V Corps Artillery, the entire TOC was captured, to include the Commanding General. There had been no warning whatsoever. The Aggressor Force of 50 soldiers, part of the 10the Special Forces Group from Bad Tolz, Germany, had parachuted into the Corps Artillery area, utilizing the High Altitude Low Opening (HALO) concept. They had exited their aircraft above 20,000 feet and had opened their chutes at 800 feet. There had been no aircraft noise and the SF personnel had not fired a shot. They had quietly overpowered the Corps security forces, tying them up and gagging them. Their professionalism so impressed him that upon completion of the maneuver, he immediately applied for Airborne School and a Special Forces assignment.

Childres graduated from the SF school at Fort Bragg the same day he received his Captain's bars. Like his fellow graduates he hoped for a Vietnam assignment where he could put to use the things he had learned.

Three months later his wish came true and he was in route to Vietnam. Because of the buildup of SF troops in VN during the fall of '64, Childres was not given the opportunity, like most of the other "A" Detachment commanders, to pick his own team, with personnel he wanted. Instead he took over an already established formed and trained team. The team was given an existing camp in the northern part of Vietnam. This in itself was a break, in that they didn't have to build new facilities and recruit mercenaries. All they had to do was improve upon what was already there. There was, however, a drawback being assigned to that particular area. The northern Corps of Vietnam was an extremely political area. Due to the distance from Saigon, whoever was the I Corps Commander ruled that region as if it was autonomous state, merely paying lip service to the Saigon government. The current Corps Commander had taken part in the suppression of the recent Montagnard uprising and recognized that the Yards had more loyalty to the Americans than they did to the Vietnamese. He therefore ordered that no Montagnard Company was to remain in one camp longer than three months at a time, but was to be rotated to another camp, to prevent them from establishing too close ties with a particular American group.

This order put a heavy administrative and logistical strain on the Special Forces camps, for along with moving the soldiers they also had to move the dependents, which usually averaged four or five people per soldier. It was also a morale factor for the soldiers and the SF team, for there was little loyalty on the soldier's part to a particular camp. The teams felt that as soon as they got to know a company well, they were transferred out. There was another factor which was peculiar to the Northern Sector of Vietnam. Instead of having perhaps two different tribes in one camp, as was the norm in Central and Southern VN, the Northern regions camps could have up to six tribes, some of which were less than friendly toward each other. Since some of the northern tribes knew no boundaries, some of the mercenaries were known border crossers and Viet Cong plants.

These were some of the problems Childres and his team faced as they took over the SF camp at Dong Da in the Northern I Corps of Vietnam. After two months on site, the VC situation had deteriorated to the point that they could not leave camp with less than a two company size force. During the first part of January 1965, the camp was hit on ten consecutive nights. The intelligence reports indicated extensive buildups in the camp area of operation.

At one of the afternoon briefings, Childres informed his team that a major attack on the camp was imminent. A Vietnamese Airborne Battalion was on standby in case the attack did come.

"Do we have any alternate plans should the weather prevent planes from getting in here?" asked Lieutenant Michalson, the team XO.

"The reaction force will use ground transportation if the weather is a factor. Of course, instead of an hour's reaction time, we're talking about three to four hours. Meanwhile, we'd better plan on escape and evasion should worse come to worse. I want you, Lt Michalson and Sgt Watson, to take a look at both the primary and alternate landing zones. Make sure they are both intact and that no one has been digging holes out there."

Childres had little faith in the Vietnamese reaction force. Two other camps had recently been overrun. In one case the Vietnamese had refused to go in and assist them; the other had gotten there too late. The American Forces Commander in Vietnam had ordered that the SF camps were not expendable; therefore a force would go to their aid.

The attack had come as predicted. First, they had received a mortar and artillery prep, and then the assault. The assault had been a halfhearted test to probe the camp's defensives. An hour after the first assault they received another heavy bombardment. Situated in the Command and Communications bunker, Childres instructed the radio operator to request assistance.

"The force is airborne - will land here within an hour," the radio operator informed him.

The shelling of the camp continued. Childres had a clear view of the Landing Zones from his location.

"We are getting a ground assault on the north side," yelled the radio operator.

Childres could see the VC hitting the outer wire, laying satchel charges and Bangalore torpedoes, to breach the wire. Most of the VC were killed, but not until the damage had been done. An explosion ripped a gap in the triple concertina wire. The Yards were fighting well, in fact better than Childres had expected.

"It looks like the main assault will be from the north side. Get some reinforcements over there." Childres directed his comments at his XO, who immediately disappeared out of the bunker. The barrage was having its desired effect on the camp's defenders, keeping them pinned in their trenches and foxholes.

The ground assault started again. The reinforcements had not gotten to the north side. The VC were now streaming through the narrow gap in the wire.

"We are getting a ground attack on the south side also," reported the radio operator.

"Well, the landing zone is still clear. When they arrive you can give them an all clear. I want someone down there to smoke it."

"I'll do it, Captain. I have selected 25 Yards to go with me to help secure it. In fact, they are standing by right now," said Sgt Powell, the Operations Sergeant.

"Good, you'd better get down there fast. They should have a visual on us soon."

The Yards were starting to withdraw from the first line of defense, and were setting up in the secondary or alternate defensive position. The VC were now inside the camp. He instructed the Engineer Sergeant to prepare the Claymore mines, which had been installed just for this type of situation.

"Sir, I've had them ready for the last five minutes."

"Okay, blow the entire north side."

The Sergeant squeezed the black handle. The VC had just started to move forward when the blast from the Claymore mines hit them with a deafening roar. There was a sudden stillness while the dust from the mines settled.

Then just as suddenly the noise started again. The VC who were still alive were trying to drag the bodies of their comrades back through the wire. The bombardment started again. The camp's bunkers and strong points were being systematically eliminated. The VC were walking their artillery and mortar rounds back and forth through the camp.

"Sir, it's the Lieutenant."

"Where the hell are you?" yelled Childres into the mike. "I told you to get the reinforcements up to the north side. Over."

There were crackling sounds on the radio as the Lieutenant started to speak. "We're pinned down here, are receiving heavy fire on the south side also. I saw the Operations Sgt take it through the chest. The VC are getting some help from some of the Yards. Several of the bunkers down here are being blown by our people. I can see the choppers coming in. Over."

"Okay, hang in there and do the best you can. Stay on the horn. Out."

Childres was getting mad. "I'm going to try and get to the L^Z," he told the Engineer Sgt. "Help me round up some soldiers to secure it."

"Got you."

"Tell the choppers what our situation is down here, and that I'm on the way to secure the Landing Zone."

"Roger sir, will do." The radio operator was transmitting his message as Childres and the Engineer Sgt left the bunker.

They had gotten about 50 feet from the command bunker

when a shell exploded next to Childres, hurling him into the air.

The helicopters started to land, about 15 of them had touched down when suddenly MG fire started crisscrossing the entire landing area. The choppers who were already on the ground were engulfed in flames and MG fire. The VC had dug positions all around the L^Z and were waiting for the soldiers jumping out of the choppers. Most were killed or wounded immediately. Some of the choppers managed to get off. The Commander of the Command and Control chopper circling overhead directed the other choppers to hold on station and not land. He immediately sent out an emergency air strike request for any planes in the region to divert to his location. Within a few seconds he received his Roger, two flights of three were on their way, station time less than five minutes.

Lt Michalson had observed the disaster on the Landing Zone. During a lull in the firing, he managed to crawl from his trench and head for the command bunker. About 50 feet from the bunker he spotted Childres lying on the ground alongside the Engineer Sgt. He quickly checked them both. The Sgt was dead. Childres was still breathing. He grabbed him by the collar and dragged him toward the bunker. The radio operator was the only one in the bunker as he dragged Childres in.

"Get the stretcher off the wall," he directed. Together they placed Childres on the stretcher and checked him for wounds.

"It looks like his legs and chest, Lt."

"Bandage him up while I see what's going on."

Lt Michalson glanced out the portholes of the bunker. The barrage had stopped. That could only mean they were about to get another ground assault. He looked around the camp. Smoke was coming from some of the buildings. Heavy black smoke was billowing from the choppers burning on the Landing Zone. Christ, what a helluva bind.

The radio startled him. It was the Command and Control

chopper. "Base, I have some birds coming in, where do you want them, over."

"This is base; give me all you have on the north and south side of the camp. They can put their stuff right on the perimeter. Over."

"Roger, request you stay on the Romeo and direct any changes, out."

The planes came in flying parallel, hitting both sides of the camp at the same time. Napalm canisters hit the perimeters engulfing the attacking VC. The second planes also dropped Napalm. The entire north and south portions of the camp were engulfed in flames.

"They are withdrawing, request you pursue them," Lt Michalson yelled over the radio.

"Roger, we see them. Out."

The attacking planes followed up their attacks on the VC with bombs and 20 mm cannon fire. The choppers that had been circling landed and the VN airborne soldiers cleaned up the small pockets of VC who were not able to escape the perimeter.

Childres' first recollection of anything was waking up in the bunker and hearing Lt Michalson directing the defense of the camp. Seeing Childres' eyes open, the radio operator asked him how he was feeling.

"My legs. What happened?"

"A shell caught you and Sgt White. He didn't make it. It's all over now. We'll have you out of here in a few minutes."

THE PIT

Spring had arrived and the weather was getting sunny and warm. The members of the "Snake Pit" were spending as much time as possible outside taking sunbaths and walking, trying to get back into some semblance of physical shape.

Pete had started jogging each day. It had been a painful experience at first, but gradually he was getting to the point where he could run half a mile without stopping. All his smaller wounds were healed, only his hand needed additional work. He had been told it would take another five or six months. He had two more bone transplants, plus some full thickness skin grafts to be done.

The wedding to Bjorkvik was coming up in a week. They had decided on a small wedding, the immediate family if they were able to make it, which was highly doubtful. Bjorkvik' father was dead, her mother had remarried and was now living in Hawaii. There had never been a close relationship between Bjorkvik and her mother so her presence was not expected.

His own family was in Europe. It looked like The Pit members and some of the doctors and nurses would be it, which was fine with both he and Bjorkvik; neither cared for large ceremonies.

The excitement of the wedding had not hit him yet. Bjorkvik, with the help of Pat, was making all of the arrangements. He had been told all he had to do was show up at the chapel.

Tom and Pat had loaned them their summer place on the beach at Kennebunkport in Maine for their week's honeymoon. It would still be a little cool up there, but he had no doubts about them staying warm.

"Has anyone noticed how quiet Pete has been the last week? You suppose maybe he's getting cold feet? Getting married is a big step, Pete. Maybe you ought to reconsider." It was Childres, trying to pull his chain again. "You know, old Bjorkvik had her eye on him from the first day she got here."

"Yah, well I guess everyone has to go sometime. We know

one thing, she really has a temper, isn't that right, Sandusky?" said John.

"You guys can't forget that, can you? I want you to know Bjorkvik and I have come to an understanding. We haven't had any problems lately. That reminds me, I got the go sign from the doc this morning. I'm going back to duty for a three month trial starting next week. I hope my arm holds up this time. I'm trying to get assigned back to an aviation detachment."

"That's great news, Sandusky," said Childres. "I hope the next guy that takes your bed has some class."

Sandusky gave him the finger.

"All kidding aside, we all hope you make it alright. You'll be the first one to go back to the real world," said John. "You will be here for Pete's wedding, won't you?"

"You bet. I wouldn't miss that for the world. All that free booze and horny nurses around. Are you kidding?"

The wedding had been nice. About forty people had shown up at the chapel, and the reception later at the Officers' Club. They had received some very nice wedding gifts, to include a chrome plated urinal made into a cocktail shaker with the names of "The Pit" members, and all the doctors and nurses who had worked on him inscribed on it. The urinal had been fitted with a top. It had been a real hit, second only to a giant three foot long condom, with an official Army identification tag, listing it as a SF issue only. Bjorkvik had received some good natured ribbing from Colonel Grange and the hospital commander.

When they left the reception at 6:00 PM, everyone had been feeling no pain. The hospital commander had given them his car and driver to take them by Bjorkvik' apartment and to their flight to Maine.

"Well, how does it feel to be married?" she had asked him on the way to the airport.

He told her he wasn't sure yet, leaning over and kissing her gently on the lips.

The honeymoon had been wonderful. He was starting to realize how lucky he was. Bjorkvik proved to be a good cook. The restaurants on the beach had not opened yet for the summer crowd, so they had bought their food at the local store. She was a very practical and loving bride.

They arrived back two days before her leave was up. Pat had moved all his belongings from "The Pit" into Bjorkvik' apartment. They found a magnum of champagne in the refrigerator, with a one word note on it, "Snake Pit."

"That was sweet of them, wasn't it?" He told her they had probably dissolved a dozen muscle relaxers in it.

"Oh come on, they wouldn't do anything like that, would they? They better not have, because your wife is in the mood for a little champagne and a lot of loving tonight. Plane rides do something to me."

He told her he would have to remember that, and kissed her.

They spent the next few days getting their finances arranged and opened joint accounts.

"How are we going to have the checks personalized? Cpt and Lt Compton, Mr. and Mrs., or what?" They finally settled on Cpt Peter and Lt Bjorkvik Compton.

One day a neatly dressed man walked into the "Snake Pit." He walked around and talked to each of them. When the man got to Pete's bed, he sat down and asked Pete if he could talk to him. The man introduced himself and said he was the president of the U.S. Junior Chamber of Commerce.

Pete asked what he could do for him

"Well, we have been thinking of some projects that would help the Vietnam people. We have several things going on to support our troops, but the Vietnam people are caught up in this war also."

Pete told him about Dr. Turpin and his small hospital up in the highlands area, west of the town of Dalat. Dr. Turpin had a staff of a French Dr. and a couple of nurses. They were always short of medical supplies. Pete had helped him whenever he could, but with almost 3,000 soldiers and dependents to take care of, there was just so much he could do.

"Dr. Turpin probably treats as many VC's as he does friendlies, but he never asks. He just administers to anyone who needs his help."

"That's just the kind of project we are looking for. What does he need?" The Jr. Chamber guy wrote as he was talking.

"Well, you can probably get a pretty good list of medicines from the hospital doctors here, but he is in desperate need of some generators – a couple of 5KW's and two or three 3KW's. He needs refrigerators to keep his medicine in and also some form of transportation. He really needs an airplane – single engine, powerful motor and space in it for transporting supplies. He is a rated pilot. So is the French doc. They have an old jeep that gets them around the immediate area, but the plane would give him access to Nha Trang and Saigon."

"Thanks, Pete. This is great and I think we can handle it." He shook Pete's hand and departed.

Pete wasn't sure Dr. Turpin would get anything. There were a lot of people who promised, but few came through with anything.

Approximately 2 ½-3 months later, a large envelope arrived for Pete. He opened it and there were a half dozen 8 x 10 color pictures and some notes inside. The first picture he saw was an American civilian standing next to Dr. Turpin next to an airplane. Pete looked at the rest of the pictures. They were all taken on Dr. Turpin's small airstrip adjacent to his hospital.

"What have you got there?" Bjorkvik had walked in and picked up the picture of the two men and the plane.

"Do you know these people?" she asked him. Pete told her the story. They looked at the other pictures together.

"Those are brand new refrigerators and look at the boxes of medicine." Bjorkvik was more excited than Pete. There were also five generators.

"Well, Dr. Turpin should be in good shape for a while," said Pete.

The notes were from Dr. Turpin, thanking Pete for thinking about him when Pete had his own problems to overcome. The other note was from the President of the Jr. Chamber of Commerce, saying "mission accomplished" and pointing out that the company that had provided the plane also had sent over a mechanic/pilot who would check out the pilots who were going to fly the plane.

"You are really something, Pete Compton," said Bjorkvik, kissing Pete's cheek and dabbing her eyes as she walked out of the "Pit."

John had been the last one to be fitted with a leg prosthesis. His long hospitalization had left him weak and soft physically. He had not been doing the exercises devised for him by the doctors and the Physical Therapy Department, so now he had to work extra hard. In addition to working with the PT clinic, he had also started staying an extra hour working out with Pete, doing sit-ups and weight lifts. He had been on this program a little over a month and was starting to feel better both physically and mentally. An hour each afternoon was spent learning how to walk with his new leg; at first between two parallel bars, and then with a cane. It would be at least one more week of practice before they would let him take the new leg back to the "Snake Pit." Adjustments were being made to the leg almost every day, until it fit him perfectly, and it was not wearing or chaffing on his stump.

He had definitely decided to stay in the Army once he was

discharged from the hospital. He had been offered a branch transfer from the Artillery to the Adjutant General Corps, which he knew he could handle even with his disability. He had not fallen in love like some of the guys. Rather, he had tried to date as many different nurses as possible, which was no easy chore, since up to now he had had to utilize his crutches wherever he went. But found most of them very understanding. In fact, most of them were too understanding, which made him feel uneasy and unsure of himself. He felt most at ease with Cpt Whealen, whom he had dated most often and had established a sort of semiserious relationship with.

As he walked into The Pit from one of his afternoon walking sessions, Childres greeted him.

"Hey John, you've got a freebie this weekend. The International Hotel downtown has invited a member of the "Snake Pit" on a weekender, and since all the others will either have had surgery or are going somewhere else, we gave them your name."

"Thanks guys, it would have been nice to have asked me first, don't you think? You know I'm getting my prosthesis for keeps on Thursday, and I was planning on throwing a little party up at the O Club Saturday night. So fuck you all. I'll just save my money."

"It'll do you good to meet some civilian broads. You haven't been out on one of these boondoggles in months," said Tom.

"Oh, the ugly Irishman is now handing out advice. You haven't been anywhere except the club and over to Pat's apartment since you got your prosthesis. Who are you to talk? Fuck you."

"Listen John, are you going or not? We have to confirm this afternoon, if you'll definitely accept or not. Their Public Relations officer will be up here Friday morning to pick you up."

"Okay you shitheads, I'll go, but from now on keep your

fucking noses out of my business."

He stomped out on his crutches. Shit, he would have to go up and get some decent clothes, which would mean taking his new leg with him, otherwise the clothes wouldn't fit right. He headed for the PT room to get his leg.

"Hey, it worked," said Tom. "It's the best thing for him to get out as soon as possible with his new leg. Believe me, it's a traumatic experience. The night Pat and I went out with Pete and Bjorkvik was my first night, and that was only down to the Fishnet Restaurant. I wasn't sure I had the guts to do it. You feel like everyone is staring and pointing at you, which they really aren't. Childres, you'd better call down to the International and make the final arrangements."

"What was the PR girl's name?" asked Childres.

"Carrie Shaw," answered Tom.

John had bought new clothes, a sports coat, slacks and shirts, and was dressed and waiting when Miss Shaw arrived Friday to pick him up.

Bjorkvik had brought her down to the "Snake Pit" and introduced her to all the men. To say she was a looker was an understatement. She was tall, with light reddish hair, and was dressed as though she had just stepped out of a Vogue advertisement.

"John, are you ready?" she said in a warm friendly manner. "I would suggest bringing an overnight bag with you if you haven't planned for it already."

"I'm all set," said John, picking up his hanging suit bag. "Let's go." He knew the "Pit" members were watching his every move and word. He led the way out of the "Snake Pit."

"Now that's what I call a weekender," said Tom. "I could go for a little action like that myself."

"I'm sure Pat will be happy to hear that," said Bjorkvik. "I'll tell her when I meet her at the commissary this afternoon."

"Oh shit, do you guys remember when Bjorkvik' name used to be Bjorkvik and how nice she used to be? Now that she finally got her hooks into poor Pete here, she's turned into a typical meddling old wife."

Kris blew Tom a kiss and walked out.

It had been a one-sided conversation riding downtown. Carrie had done the talking and John had listened.

"I hope you don't mind if we take some pictures of you this weekend. Our publicity department likes to record these events and to be quite frank, we use it for our tax write offs."

"Sure, be my guest. It's your show. Do you want me to remove my artificial leg also?" he said sarcastically.

"No, that won't be necessary, John. I'll make it as painless as possible. My job is to see to it that you have an enjoyable weekend. You can do whatever you please."

"Will you be around all the time?"

"Well, yes. I do have to take a quick trip out to the airport tomorrow night to pick up my boyfriend." As she said this she looked at him to see if there was any reaction. "He has been out of town for a while."

"Listen, Carrie, I don't want to ruin your weekend. You just drop me off wherever, and I'll fend for myself."

"We'll see....here we are. I'll take you up to your room and get you settled and we'll have a little lunch at which time we can go over the itinerary for the next few days."

John was impressed. He had been given a beautiful suite on the top floor. Carrie had pulled back the drapes from the windows, which covered two of the walls. The view of the city was spectacular.

"Freshen up a little, and I'll meet you downstairs in the lobby in fifteen minutes. Oh, by the way, there is a small bar in the wall over there. Help yourself." Carrie walked out and closed the door behind her.

Christ, what a layout, he thought. He walked over and looked at the long paneled cabinet. He pulled the handle. "Holy shit," he said out loud. The entire section of paneling swung out on wheels and revealed a well-stocked bar, with every type of bottle imaginable.

He took a glass down and filled it with ice from the refrigerated ice container and poured a generous portion of vodka into it. This might not be a bad weekend after all.

He gulped down the drink, feeling the warm effect. He wasn't sure what to make of Carrie. He certainly didn't want to sit around hearing about her boyfriend all weekend. Christ, what a hunk of a woman. He wondered by she wasn't a model or in the movies. Certainly she could do a lot better than a PR person for a hotel. Oh well, he would play it cool and see what developed. He definitely wanted a little action this weekend, even if he had to go down to 14th street and pick something up.

He put his empty glass on the bar, and walked over to the wall length mirror for a quick inspection. When he was standing still, no one could guess that his leg was not real. The tailor had done a good job on his slacks. He was glad he had bought several pairs. Satisfied that he looked okay, he walked out and found the elevator. Carrie was waiting for him in the lobby.

"John, I want you to meet Julie Livingston. Julie, this is John Snyder."

"Hi Julie, I'm pleased to meet you."

"Likewise, I'm sure," said Julie, in a thick English accent.

"Julie has just joined our staff from our hotel in London," said Carrie . "She's working with me this week."

"Yes, and I'm learning so much. Next week will be a frightful bore, I'm afraid. I shall then be learning how the kitchen works."

As she led them into the dining room, Carrie explained that it was the hotel's procedure, when a new person joined the staff, to learn a little bit about the entire operation of the hotel. "Eventually Julie will work in our public relations department."

The head waiter led them to a table by the window which looked out over the hotel's glass bubble enclosed pool. Carrie explained it was the only year round pool in the city. The bubble separated, so when it got really warm, the bubble was removed.

He ordered a martini. The girls had whiskey sours. Carrie outlined the plan for the weekend. They would attend the hotel's show that evening, followed by a late supper. Then if he still felt like it, she knew of a nice new club about a block away, whose show he might enjoy. The next day there was a trip to the Smithsonian and dinner at the hotel. The night was up to him, anything he wanted to see or do. Sunday there was a late brunch and just relaxing.

"How does it sound, John? Have I over planned, or do you agree?"

"It sounds great. I'm a very easy person to please. So whatever you have laid on, I'm game. I don't want to take all of your time, though. I can amuse myself, and don't forget about your boyfriend coming in tomorrow night."

A puzzled look appeared on Julie's face. She looked at Carrie questioningly.

"Don't worry about that, John," Carrie quickly retorted. "I see our photographer is heading this way. You won't mind his taking a few pictures, will you?"

"Shoot away. Tell me what you want me to do."

The photographer took about six shots, finished and then departed.

The other guests in the dining room were now looking at their table, trying to figure out if they were celebrities.

"I do think we are the center of attention at the moment," said Julie. "It does make one feel rather important having one's picture taken in a public place, doesn't it?"

"Well, let's play the role. This doesn't happen too often, at least not to me," said John. He actually felt a little strange with everyone looking over at them. He took another sip of his martini and felt a little better.

Carrie was talking about a group of congressmen they had staying there last week. His mind drifted and was examining Julie. She was smaller than Carrie-he guessed her to be about 5'4", with long dark hair. She had a pert little cheer face. She wore a suite and from what he could determine had a nice build.

"Does anyone care for dessert?" said Carrie, "or maybe another drink?"

"That would be nice," said Julie. "I do think I would like another, same as this one. It's rather good, you know."

John could feel the second martini hitting him. He'd better not have another. He would hate to fall in front of everyone. "I'm fine. I'll just nurse this one along. After all, I've had two to your one," he told them.

Carrie had ordered and then signed the bill. "I have to make a run over to my place," she said, when everyone was done. "Do you want to come along for the ride, John?"

"Sure, a little fresh air will do wonders for me. How about you, Julie?" he asked.

"No thank you, I have to beg off. I have some work to do. I will see you later, though."

They had left Julie at the front desk of the hotel.

"Don't you have to work or do something back there?"

"No, this is my only job this weekend. The boss's instructions were to insure that the soldier has a good time, we can't do enough for our fighting men, quote unquote."

"I think I like your boss. I hope I get to meet him," John said with a smile.

They arrived in a tree shaded section of town. The apartment building looked old, but well kept up. He noticed the cars parked at the curb, and got the feeling he was in an upper crust neighborhood.

"Come on in," she said, getting out of the car.

He went to open the door for her, but an older man in uniform stepped out and held the door for them.

"Good afternoon, Miss Shaw."

"Good afternoon, Charlie. How are things going today?"

"Just fine, thank you," he said, touching his hat.

"It looks like you live right," he told her as they were going up in the elevator.

"Yes, I splurged on this place, but it's well worth it. I really enjoy my apartment."

He could see why, as she opened the heavy carved door for him. The apartment was done in a heavy Spanish motif, large wood and leather Spanish type furniture. In addition to a large living room, dining room combination, there were two bedrooms and a larger paneled den with a sizable collection of bound books.

"This is my favorite room" she said surveying the den. "The books and chair and desk belonged to my father. He was a judge back in Ohio, but also had an office here. In fact most of the things in this room I took from his study after he died. Sit down."

"How come you didn't follow in his footsteps? You sound like you admired him a lot."

"Oh, I did. He practically raised me. I never knew my mother. She and my only brother died in an automobile accident when I was two years old. My father never remarried. His sister came to live with us, but I was a daddy's girl; went with him on many of his travels."

"That must have been kind of rough on your father, living alone without a wife..."

"Oh, don't get me wrong, he had his women friends. Here, have a little cognac." She poured from a crystal container into two wide cognac tumblers and handed him one. "In fact when I first realized he was seeing other women I was really hurt. I think I was about fifteen at the time. But he had a way of explaining things, so I got over it. He was in the JAG Corps during WWII. In fact, that's a picture of him in his uniform. " She pointed to the opposite wall.

"He was a handsome man," he said, getting up and going over to get a closer look.

"Thank you. There is a striking resemblance between you two," she said, getting up and going over to him. "You see, he lost his leg below the knee when the jeep he was riding in over in France hit a mine."

He looked at the picture again. The man in the picture was tall and brawny, dressed in the old Army brown dress jacket and pinkish trousers. He suddenly realized that Carrie was standing close to him, her left shoulder slightly touching his back. He became uneasy. She was still talking about her father. He felt their bodies touching.

What the hell, was his imagination running away with him? It must be the cognac, he thought. After all, hadn't she told him she had a boyfriend? He turned ever so slightly, half facing her. She made no attempt to move. His arm brushed slightly against her right breast as he turned completely around.

She had stopped talking. He looked directly into her eyes, not saying a word. She returned his stare.

"Carrie," he finally managed to get out, "you are an extremely attractive and desirable girl."

She stood not moving and kept looking at him. Her breathing was becoming heavier.

"I don't know if I'm reading you right." He leaned over and kissed her lips lightly. She moved in close and put her arms around him, returning the kiss. They both still had their drinks in their hands. He kissed her deeply, feeling his drink spilling over his hand.

"Love me, John, please love me," she whispered in his ear. Her body was moving slowly against him.

He gently pushed her away, taking her drink and putting both glasses down. "Carrie, I don't know if you realize," he started to say.

"I know everything," she said, leading him by the hand over to the couch.

They kissed and gently caressed each other.

"God, I want you, John." She leaned him back, lying on top of him, moving her hips in a slow rhythm against him. His leg hit the floor with a thump. She didn't seem to notice. She was now lying between his legs, still kissing him and moving her body back and forth. He reached around her back and unbuttoned her blouse, pulling it forward. She raised herself so he could pull it free of her arms. She reached down to her side and undid her zipper on her skirt, at the same time getting up and stepping out of it. She was standing in front of him in her bra and panties and stockings.

"Come here, John," she said in a low voice. He raised himself from the couch and stood up. She took his jacket and shirt off and laid them on the couch. She undid his belt and zipper and lowered his trousers to the floor.

"Step out of them, we don't want to get them all wrinkled."

He was unsure of the next step. The shoe on his left leg as attached to the prosthesis.

"Take it all off, John." She was demanding now. He removed his leg and the rest of his clothes. She had removed her under things already.

"Come on, John, I can't wait much longer." She lay down on the soft shaggy carpet and beckoned him to come to her.

"I want it all, John." She was moaning now and rubbing her body all over him. He moved his hand between her legs. She was eager for his caresses.

"Do it, do it now. I can't wait." She rolled off him and pulled him on top of her. He felt himself going into her slowly. She wrapped her long legs around him, holding him. "Stay in me for a while," she whispered.

His heart was pounding, was this really happening or was he dreaming? She started moving her hips slowly at first, then quickening the pace. Her nails were digging into his back.

"More, John, more please, faster."

Their bodies were entwined like two combatants. It was more of a battle than lovemaking. He felt himself exploding inside her. She screamed, hugging her body to him. She slowed her movements, sobbing and kissing his face, until finally she let out a deep sigh and lay still.

He moved inside her in a gentle motion. She lay completely still with her eyes closed. He slowly withdrew out of her. She opened her eyes and smiled at him, pulling his head down, kissing him softly on the forehead.

"You are really something. I'm not letting you out of here all weekend."

"I might take you up on that." He rolled over on his side next to her. She placed her hands between his legs and fondled him. "John, you are some guy. Look, he is getting ready again," she said, looking at his slowly revitalizing erection. Let's move into the bedroom."

They made love again. This time more slowly and gently. She was a magnificent girl; he was having a hard time believing all this was really happening to him. She seemed to accept his deformity without any hang-ups. They were lying in bed naked.

"How about a little more cognac," she said, getting up and

returning with just one glass. "We'll share," she said smiling at him.

"Sure," he folded his arms behind his head and lay watching her. Her long shapely legs, well-proportioned buttocks and firm pointed breasts. What the hell was she doing here making love to a messed up guy like himself? Was it part of the job?

"Here you go," handing him the glass, she laid down on her side facing him, hand under her head. "Here is to the weekend."

They took a long sip and put the glass down between them.

"We're going to have to make some of the events I outlined to you earlier, but we can cut out part of it. What do you think?"

"Carrie, I like the events so far," he said with a smile. "Whatever you have to do is fine with me. I have a nice room over at the hotel. We have to use that a little too, you know."

"That's a problem. We have to be very discreet. It's frowned on for the PR chief to shack up with hotel guests. So we probably shouldn't be seen going up there together, as silly as it sounds."

"As long as we both know the ground rules, that's the important thing. I don't want to jeopardize your job, but it would be nice to be together tonight."

"We will, you can be sure of that."

"What about your boyfriend tomorrow night?"

She smiled at him and took a sip of the drink. "There is no boyfriend. I tell guys that to keep them from coming on too strong. It works wonders. The guy I was engaged to was killed in 1963 in route to Vietnam. You might remember the chartered plane carrying US advisors that went down in the Pacific. We were planning on marrying when he got back. Since then, there haven't been any boyfriends."

"I'm sorry, it sounds like you were very close."

"Yes, about as close as two people could possibly be. I

stayed with him while he was going through training at Fort Benning, and later at Fort Bragg. Anyway, that's all in the past, and you're stuck with me this weekend."

"Well, I can struggle through anything," he said, putting his hand on her hip.

"You know, I have to tell you something else. This was not in my plans this weekend. I don't know what happened, but something just came over me. My nickname at work runs from iceberg to frigid to gay. Maybe it was just the time and the circumstances. What I wanted to tell you was that Julie had volunteered to show you a good time. You might say she is a little more liberated than me, although I wonder about that too, after the session we've just had. We'll have to give her some type of explanation. Or maybe you would like a little variety," she said with a questioning look on her face.

He moved his hand over her hip and up to her breast. "Carrie, I'm very pleased and happy. I couldn't think of a nicer way to spend the weekend, or with a nicer and more beautiful girl." He leaned over and kissed her breast.

"Honey, remarks like that will get you anything. You know, I'm starving. Let's get dressed and head back to the hotel for a nice dinner, okay?"

"Lead the way."

"I'm going to take a quick shower, what about you?"

"Is that an invitation?"

"Well, when was the last time you had your back washed? Never mind, come on."

He had leaned on her going into the shower. He felt kind of ridiculous hopping along on one leg, but Carrie didn't seem to mind at all. They had washed each other and it soon became obvious that both were ready to make love. They started kissing with water running down their faces and bodies.

"John, can we make it?" She took him in her hand, spreading her legs and bending them slightly, and guided him into her with some difficulty.

"Oh God, hang on to me," she moaned, moving her hips back and forth. She arched her back, making a final thrust with her hips, letting out a cry.

"We must be a little crazy," she said, holding him close, not moving. He kissed the top of her head.

"Now I'm getting hungry," he said, gently pushing her away.

"Enough of this, Mr. Snyder, you're spoiling me." She turned off the shower and started toweling him off. When he was dry, he hobbled out to the den and started getting dressed. He could hear her hair dryer going.

What a girl, he thought to himself. The thought of two nights with her made his pulse quicken. He finished dressing and was combing his hair when she came out wearing a slip.

"Do you want some of this?" she said, holding up a can of talcum powder. "My father had to use it all the time."

"Thanks, you're absolutely right. I guess my mind was on other things."

"Now, now, must take care of first things first." She helped him off with his artificial leg and sprinkled a generous portion of talcum into the hollowed out portion that his stump fitted into.

"That should do it," she said, holding the artificial leg for him while he inserted his leg into it.

"You are a remarkable girl, Carrie."

"Oh, you'd be surprised at the talents I have. You ain't seen nothing yet, mister."

They drove back to the hotel, going directly to the dining room. The waiter gave them the same table they had for lunch.

"Do you realize it's after seven? Where has the afternoon gone? No wonder I'm so starved."

"Well, you know the old saying about time flying when you're having fun."

"John," she said, putting her hand over his, "I really had the most fantastic time of my life this afternoon. I really mean that."

"Hi there, I've been looking for you two." Julie had walked up unnoticed. She cast a quick glance at Carrie's hand on top of John's.

"Sit down Julie," John said, starting to get up.

"No, please don't bother, I can't stop. I just wanted to ask if I could beg off tonight, Carrie. You see, some dear friends arrived this afternoon and....

"It's fine, Julie. I'll see you tomorrow."

"Then I'll leave you two." She walked off.

"That girl is pretty smart. She knows exactly what happened this afternoon."

"Yes, I'm afraid you're right. Is it that obvious? Does it show?"

"Well, your cheeks are a little rosy, and your eyes are a little, well I don't know how to describe them."

"Bright, shining, happy looking?"

"Yes, maybe."

The waiter walked up and they ordered their drinks and dinner.

"Cheers again." He held up his glass to hers.

"Cheers, John."

The dinner was consumed in almost total silence. They both ate ravenously.

"Wow, I didn't think I was going to get enough," Carrie said. "What would you like to do next?"

"Would it mess things up if we just went upstairs, put our feet up and sipped some of that nice cognac I saw in the bar, and just watched the lights of the city?"

"I'm sold. I'll just stop by the office and leave a note. You go on up . I'll be there in a few minutes."

They both got up and she reached over and squeezed his hand. He walked slowly out of the dining room over to the elevator. He was tired and he could feel the nerve endings on his stump throbbing. He pushed the button for his floor. In a few seconds he arrived and was unlocking his door.

He didn't realize that lovemaking could fatigue him so. She was a very demanding girl, but wonderful. He took off his tie and jacket and hung them up. He moved two of the footstools over in front of the overstuff sofa.

He pushed the buttons for classical music and turned it down low. What a beautiful place, he thought. He went to sit down when he remembered the bottle of cognac. Going over to the bar, he selected the smoky green bottle of Courvoisier Napoleon cognac which he knew to be at least 25 years old. Oh well, the hotel wouldn't have put it there if they didn't want it tasted.

He poured two generous helpings into the tumblers and placed the glasses and bottle on the table next to the couch. Sitting down, he put his feet up on the footstool.

The lights of the city were below him. He could see the Capitol building all lit up. He must have dozed. Through half-opened eyes he saw Carrie coming around the front of the couch. He pretended he was sleeping. She took some pillows from a chair and gently lifted his amputated leg off the foot stool. She pushed up his trousers, gently removing the artificial leg, placing the stump on the pillows she had placed on the foot stool. This elevated his leg a little. He noticed she had removed her dress and was wearing only a man's loose silk robe. As she sat down quietly next to him, he leaned his head over toward her and said, "I think I love you."

"You're awake? I was trying to be very quiet and careful so

as not to disturb you. I didn't make it."

"Did you hear what I said?"

"I'm afraid to hear you. Can you understand that?" She had a faraway look in her eyes.

"I guess I do," he said, taking her hand and squeezing it.

"I brought you a present. I'm not sure you smoke, but I brought you these." She held up five cigars. He took one from her and examined it. He recognized the brand.

"You can't buy these around most places. Is this by any chance the brand your father smoked?"

"Yes, how did you know that?"

"Oh, a lucky guess, you might say." He handed her one of the glasses of cognac and she snuggled up to him on the couch.

"Thanks, Carrie, I will treasure these." Leaning over, he kissed the top of her head.

They sat in silence, sipping the drinks. He removed the cellophane from a cigar and lit it up.

"I love that fragrance," she said.

He held the cigar down to her indicating she take a drag.

She took a small puff and immediately blew out the smoke. "It tastes kind of mild, doesn't it?" she said, running her tongue over her lips.

"It's the best there is. Your father had good taste. Not to mention a beautiful daughter."

"Keep it up. Talk like that will get you a nice romp in the bed tonight."

"I was kind of hoping you would say that."

They sipped their drinks in silence. He moved his hand down her shoulder and along her side to her hip. He could feel her firm body underneath the thin silk robe.

"I'm naked underneath, you know."

"You feel good."

"Do I shock you, John? Am I being too pushy?"

"Not at all, I'd be dressed the same way if I had a robe like that."

She got up and went into the bedroom, reappearing with a matching robe.

"When I plan, I plan," she said, throwing the robe over his head.

"Let me help you." She undressed him, taking his clothes and hanging them up in the closet.

"Give me the stocking you wear on your leg." He removed the orthopedic stocking from his stump, and handed it to her. She disappeared into the bathroom. He heard her filling the sink. My God, she knew about the cleaning of the stocking. She returned in a few minutes.

"I used to do it all the time for my father. It will be dry in the morning."

It was April and the weather was getting balmy.

"You know, we've been talking about going sailing and all we've done is talk. We haven't left this place. No one is scheduled for surgery, so how about going down to the bay and renting a boat tomorrow?" said Tom.

"Tomorrow is kind of sudden, isn't it, Tom? We should really plan this. After all, no one really knows much about sailing."

"Hey, wait a minute, Childres, I sailed for over three years, twice a week, even got my coast guard license. And besides, Tom grew up on the ocean and has sailed since he was a kid," John said, kind of annoyed.

"Okay then, let's go. Doc Berg goes down to a place called Jones Dock on weekends. I'll get the directions. I think he said it was $30 for a 26 footer. Hell, split six ways that's not bad," said Tom.

The more they talked about it the more excited they got. Pat and Kris had packed a lunch for them, and George and

Childres had procured a cooler full of beer. Tom's station wagon was pressed into service. It was decided that they would remove their prostheses in case they fell overboard. So the wheelchairs were collapsed and loaded into the back of the wagon. Childres and Pete were the only ones with two good legs. Both Steve and George had new casts on that went almost to their knees.

They had found Jones Dock after stopping a few times and asking directions. Childres was elected spokesman and money handler, so it was he who presented himself at the small shack which acted as the rental office. A large sign erected in the form of an archway announced that boats were available by day or week for leasing, giving the cost by the size of the boat. Beyond the shack and sign was an extensive docking area with perhaps 20 to 30 boats, ranging in size from 12 to 35 feet.

"Can I help you?" the voice came from the open window that served as the transaction place.

"Yes, I would like to rent one of your 26 footers," said Childres.

"Okay, fill out everything on this form, and don't forget to list the names of all the people going with you. It's a coast guard regulation in case anything happens. Not that I expect anything to happen, but you never know."

The man speaking was fat and already perspiring from the morning heat. A can of beer was firmly emplaced in his left hand.

Childres filled out the form. Handing it back to the man behind the window, he asked how much it was for the day.

"That'll be $30, plus your driver's license. It's sort of collateral and also a coast guard regulation."

Childres handed him the money and the driver's license.

"Okay, I assume you know how to handle the boat. The life preservers are in the forward hatch. Have a good sail."

The man handling the transaction up to this time had

only seen Childres. The others had been lined up on a narrow board walk, single file, leading up to the parking area. George on crutches and Tom and John in wheelchairs. As they started filing past the shack, the man inside looked out with an exasperated look on his face.

"Hey, come back here," he yelled at Childres. "You can't take those people on my boat! What the hell are you trying to do, have my license revoked?"

Childres walked back and was standing by the window. "I rented the boat from you and gave you the money. What more do you want? As far as I'm concerned we have a deal."

"Not on your ass, young fellow." The fat man was starting to get excited. "I can't let them on my boat, they don't have any legs and the others have casts. It's a coast guard regulation."

"You show me where it says that a person has to have two legs and can't have a cast on in order to go sailing." Childres was getting hot under the collar.

The fat man was by now fuming. "Maybe it doesn't say exactly that, but I have a rule here which says I can refuse service to anyone I want to." He was waving the beer can around, spilling some of the contents over the paperwork strewn over his desk.

"Okay, that's fine," said John, in a calm voice. "But I can assure you, Mr. Jones, that I will report this to my cousin, Jack Anderson. You know who he is, don't you? He writes for Drew Pearson.

"Don't give me that crap. Jack Anderson is no more your cousin than he is mine."

"Did you by any chance read the story about the hospital he did? Well, he was over visiting me at the hospital when he noticed the deplorable conditions. And you have to admit he got the government and the Army off their cans and got some action."

"Come on, you can't tell me he is your cousin."

"Well, we will see, Mr. Jones. You are Mr. Jones, are you not?"

"Yah, I'm Mr. Jones, the owner."

"Well, we'll see how long you remain the owner after Jack lets the rest of the nation know how you refused to rent a boat to wounded Vietnam veterans. Not to mention what the VFW and the American Legion will do." John started wheeling himself up the boardwalk to where the car was parked.

"Hey, you, wait a minute," the fat man Mr. Jones was perspiring profusely by now.

"Oh, by the way, Mr. Jones," It was Childres' turn. "You may have read in the papers where wounded Vietnam veterans are often asked to speak at various civic organizations, VFW, American Legion, Lions, etcetera. Well, check the names in the papers with the ones listed on the form I filled out. I think you will find they are the same."

"Okay, come back here, maybe I was a little hasty. Here, take these extra life preservers." He started throwing preservers out the window. "And make sure you put them on."

John had turned around and was next to the window. "Look, Mr. Jones, we just want to do some sailing. Most of us have been in the hospital for over a year, we need to get out of there before we go crazy. We know how to sail, and will take good care of your boat."

"Yeah, I was a little hasty, I guess. You didn't have to pull that Jack Anderson stuff with me, though. Now, admit it, he isn't your cousin, is he?"

John looked him in the eyes. "I can assure you, Mr. Jones, he is who I said he was and will be over to see me this weekend."

"Okay, I believe you. Here, it's a little discount for you boys." He handed John a ten dollar bill. "If you need a boat in the future, just let me know. Give me a call." Mr. Jones waved them on.

They got the boat out and the sails hoisted; John took the tiller and directed everyone else on what to do. It was a beautiful day with a brisk wind. John proved to be a good instructor and gave everyone a chance at the tiller. They had passed the old naval point and were cruising out into the Chesapeake Bay. Tom was instructing everyone on the buoys and markers.

"What would you have done if Jones called your bluff on Anderson?" asked Tom.

"Oh, I don't know. I suppose I would have called him up. I think he would have gone along with us."

"I think John is right," said George. Anderson would have backed us."

They had settled down and eaten the sandwiches and drank some beer. George was having a little trouble with the tiller.

"You are making too much of a correction, George. Pretend you are flying your chopper. Anticipate the boat and make smaller corrections," John said, obviously enjoying his role as instructor. They were in the middle of the bay when John gave the order to lower the sails.

"What's up?" Childres asked, as he lowered the forward sail.

"Never mind, do as I say and you'll see." With the sails down the boat just drifted with the current.

"Here you are." John reached into the bag he had carried with him and handed each one a small hand held fishing reel with lines, hooks and sinkers on them. He reached into the cooler and unwrapped a newspaper package containing shrimp. Handing out the bait, he instructed them to lower the lines about thirty feet. They had waited only a few minutes when Childres announced he had one on. Hauling in the line he displayed a ten inch bass. Soon everyone was catching fish, bass but mostly brim.

"Put them in the cooler with the beer," said John. "It won't hurt the beer. We'll stop when we get to a hundred. Most of them are small, so we'll need quite a few. When we run out of shrimp for bait, just cut up one of the big fish."

Everyone laughed at him. "I'll be happy if I catch one more," said Jim, "never mind a hundred."

After another hour John informed them that they had to drink the rest of the beer, because the cooler was needed for the fish.

"Hey, I think we're getting pretty close to the mark," said George. "I've never seen so much fish."

"Here is what we do, we each catch three more, then hoist the sails and head for home. Tom, you show these guys how to clean them. I'll take the tiller."

After everyone had caught the new limit, they headed back towards Jones Dock.

"It should take us over an hour to reach the dock, so all the fish should be cleaned by then. Just make sure we get all the fish in the cooler, and wash off the topsides so there's no trace of the fish," said John, bringing the boat around and setting course for home.

Everyone bitched good naturedly about the fish cleaning.

"Well, we have exactly 93," said Childres, after the last fish had been cleaned.

"What are we going to do with them all?" asked George.

"We're going to have a fish fry. We'll let the girls get some goodies together and we'll cook the fish," said John. "We'll call them from the dock and give them a warning order."

"I think Pete better talk nice to Kris, since their place is the biggest," said John.

He had told them it would be all right. Kris was a fish eater and would enjoy it. They planned the fish party and everyone would contribute.

By the time they reached the dock, the boat was cleaned and the life preservers stowed away in the forward hatch.

Jones welcomed them as they tied up, obviously with a sign of relief upon seeing that everyone was present and his boat in good shape. Childres handed Jones the cooler full of fish.

"You boys didn't drink much beer. It feels like it's still full," said Jones, grunting at the weight.

"We don't drink beer on the boat. Only took coke with us, and no one was too thirsty," said John.

"That's a damn good idea. You shouldn't drink when you sail. Most of my customers come back half stiff."

"Well, we know the Coast Guard regulations," said Childres, taking one handle of the cooler and indicating to Pete to take the other.

"We'll see you again next week, Mr. Jones. Take care now," said John, getting into his wheel chair, and wheeling himself up the incline to the station wagon. They had all said goodbye to Mr. Jones, who had stood staring after them scratching his head.

The girls had all brought something and the fish fry was a success. John and Pete did the frying and George tended the bar.

"How is everything going?" asked Kris, coming into the kitchen with a drink for them. "I don't think you should fry anymore. Everyone is getting stuffed. Just fry enough for the two of you."

"Okay, got you," said John. "We'll be there in a few minutes."

"Before you go, you might as well wrap the rest of the fish up and put them in the freezer," said John.

As John and Pete walked into the living room, everyone made a big fuss over them and their cooking ability. As usual when they got together, everyone was getting a little happy.

"I have to work tomorrow," said Whealen. "I'd better call it a night. John, are you about ready?" John swallowed his drink and indicated in the affirmative.

"See you all at rounds in the morning," said John, leaning down and giving Kris a kiss on the cheek. "You're a real sport, I promise we won't switch beds on you anymore." John was slurring his words, a sure indicator that he was reaching his limit.

"John Snyder, do you remember the oath you guys took that day about not mentioning that incident again?" said Kris, getting up and pushing him toward the door.

"I'm sorry, kid, you know me. I'm basically a liar. Never trust an SF man." He waved at the others and departed. Kris closed the door after them. "John has not been the same since he came back from that weekend at the International," said Tom.

"I know," said Linda, "Whealen has talked to me about it several times. She's really stuck on the guy. I guess Miss Shaw must be some girl."

"Leave him alone," said Jim. "Let's not get into the matchmaking game. I happen to know he is really serious about Carrie. They hit it off good. It's the first girl he has really been serious about."

"Now you just wait a minute, Jim." Linda was getting mad. "Whealen has really taken care of him, I mean really taken care of him. I think he owes her something."

"Hey, come on. There are no secrets in the "Snake Pit." We all know that she has been screwing him. She's a big girl; it doesn't mean she owns him. I'm sure she enjoyed it as much as him," said Tom.

"You just wait a minute, Tom. You're getting drunk. It's not that easy for Whealen to go to bed with a guy like John."

"Oh shit, Pat, you broads are all alike. You think just because you're women, you're something special."

"Tom Connor, you are in trouble and better be quiet," said Pat.

Pat got up and said good night to everyone and said how much she had enjoyed it. Jim and Childres got up also and bade farewell.

"You really made a fool of yourself tonight, Tom," said Pat, getting up and picking up the dishes.

"Why is everyone getting so excited, Pete? Just because a girl screws a guy, doesn't mean she owns him, right Perez?"

"I agree, Tom. You have to reach an understanding before you go to bed with a guy. If you start attaching strings to your lovemaking you take all the fun and pleasure out of it," said Perez.

"Hey, I like you," said Tom. "You are the only sensible girl here. Even Kris is pissed at me, aren't you Kris?"

"No, I'm not mad at you. I think it's an individual thing, Tom. You can't lump all relationships together. They're all different."

"I hate to leave you with the dishes, but I'd better take this guy home," said Pat.

"That's all right, I'm off tomorrow."

"Oh shit, I'm not going home to our place. I'm going to the "Snake Pit." I'm not in the mood for any fucking lectures tonight. Maybe Mrs. Foster will take care of me," said Tom, laughing.

"We'd better go, too," said Perez. "Come on, George."

When everyone had left, Kris sat down on the sofa. "Get me a drink, will you, Pete?"

He fixed them both a drink and sat down next to her.

"That was an interesting conversation. Did you feel I trapped you because I went to bed with you?" she said, looking at him.

He told her no, but that it was nice to get a sample of what he was getting before they tied the knot.

"I don't know how to take that. But I'll give you the benefit of the doubt. Besides, your wife is in the mood for a little loving tonight."

One day a young man with a guitar slung across his shoulders, walked into the "Snake Pit." He introduced himself as George Santos and walked around and shook each member's hand.

"I take some college classes at Georgetown with one of the nurses here, and she told me about the "Snake Pit." I'm sure she exaggerated some of the stories of what transpires here. After all, this IS a hospital."

The members of the "Snake Pit" looked at each other and back at Santos who had made himself comfortable at the "Pit" table.

"What nurse are you taking classes with?" John asked, with a skeptical look on his face.

"She works up in the oncology or cancer ward. Her name I'd rather not say, but she indicated you might like to hear a few songs to get your minds off your problems." And having said that, Santos started strumming his guitar.

"Hey, before you start, Mr. Santos, we are pretty particular about our music. This isn't going to be some religious rendition where you try to convert us and we end up giving up alcohol and wild women. We are a pretty opinionated group here, Mr. Santos, so we don't want to waste your time if you are religiously afflicted." John was giving Santos a hard look.

'Well, why don't I start out with a few songs, and if you don't like them, you can kick me out. Is that fair enough?"

"You play whatever you want," said Tom. "John only knows two songs. 'The Ballad of the Green Berets' and 'The A-Team.'"

Santos nodded and started with the "Green Beret" song. John was in seventh heaven. Not only could Santos play a great guitar, but his voice was fantastic. Everyone clapped and John whistled when he finished. Santos went through about 5-6 songs and received loud applause.

"For those of you who are thinking of starting to go to church again and giving up your sinful ways, I have a special one for you." There was much booing and laughing.

Santos started a song that was anything but religious. It could have gotten him kicked out of the hospital if the head nurse had been present. But fortunately, there was only Kris, learning against the door along with Patients from the other rooms.

When Santos was finished everyone asked for more, but Pete held up his hand and asked Santos how much time he had.

"Oh, I can probably stay another 45 minutes to an hour. What did you have in mind?"

"Not that we don't appreciate your music, but we have a lot of enlisted men in the back wards who would welcome your talent, and believe me some of them need to get their minds off their problems."

The rest of the "Snake Pit" members agreed, and Pete volunteered to take Santos up there.

The "Pit" members thanked Santos and told him he was welcome back any time. Pete took Santos up to the enlisted ward to one of the larger rooms. He talked to their nurse and introduced Santos to her.

"You take Mr. Santos in and introduce him. It will go over better than if I do it, Pete, and they have known you for a long time."

Pete introduced Santos to the troops, and like the "Snake Pit," the patients were a little skeptical of him. However, once he started playing and singing, their mood changed. He asked for their favorites and sang them. Patients were coming from other rooms and sat on the floor or in wheelchairs and enjoyed the show.

Santos spent about an hour there. When it was over and

time to go, several of the patients gave him their Army unit patches and asked him to come back.

Pete walked Santos out to his car and asked about a return engagement.

"I can probably do it once or twice a week, but I better start with the enlisted section. They seem a little more down, and these patches they gave me really got to me."

"Yes, I know what you mean," said Pete.

True to his word, Santos returned at least once a week and word spread and the audience grew.

Gen. Myers came down to the "Snake Pit" and thanked them for sending Santos up to the enlisted ward.

"Morale is up 100%," he said and thanked the "Snake Pit" members again and left.

"We've got a new man coming in," said Tom, walking into the "Snake Pit." "He just got back from Nam, doesn't look too bad off. At least he's mobile."

"How do you know he's coming down here?" asked Jim.

"Kris is processing him in, and introduced him to me. He's a Captain and was an advisor up in I corps. Name is Brandon, or Brandon, couldn't hear him too good."

"Guys, I have a new member for you," said Kris, holding the doors open for a slight young man on crutches, and a cast up to his knee. "This is Captain Bill Brandon, just returned from Vietnam." Kris introduced him to everyone while she was folding down his bed.

"Good to see you guys, and happy to be here, I can assure you," Bill said, in a southern drawl. "By the way, are you two related?" He asked Kris, pointing to her name tag and looking over at Pete.

"Don't tell anyone, but he's my husband," said Kris with a smile.

"Well, I'll be darned. The Army really does try to station

married folks together, don't they? Well, I'll be darned. You sure you ain't trying to josh old Bill here?"

"No, I wouldn't try to josh you, Bill. We were married three months ago. I'll be back to see you in a few minutes," said Kris as she walked out the door.

Bill looked to be about 5'4", and didn't weigh more than about a hundred pounds. He looked old for a captain – probably came up through the enlisted ranks. He had been hit while he was on an operation with a Vietnamese Ranger Battalion. The bullet had shattered his ankle.

"I thought I had lost my leg, which really would have killed me. The Doc told me they would fix it up fine here. I couldn't stand the thought of losing a limb of any kind. Can you imagine the thought of going through life without an arm or a leg?"

"No, I couldn't. Imagine losing an arm or a leg?" said John, walking out the door. John and Tom both had their prosthesis on and Bill had not noticed a thing.

"I'm just an old country boy, but I know when I have offended someone. Why did he get mad? What's his name again?"

"That's John," said Tom.

"Yah, John. Why did he walk out huffy like? Did I say something wrong?"

"Look Bill," said Childres, "Most of the guys in here have been here close to a year or more. John and Tom have both lost legs; Jim lost part of his hand and Pete over there almost lost his hand. George and I were the lucky ones. We just got some leg wounds. You'll find out that to lose a limb is not the end of the world. Believe me, we do everything around here, from sailing to getting into fights down on 14th street."

"I didn't know. Tom, you'll just have to forgive this old country boy for talking too much. I guess I'm still a little scared."

"Don't worry, everyone goes through the state. And don't

worry about John and me. We have both heard what you said before. I guess it's time for my walking lesson," said Tom, and he walked out the door.

They had talked about mutual places and common friends. Pete had told him he had been up in his area last year. The more Bill talked, the more obvious it became just how worried he was about his wound, and staying in the Army. The Army was the only thing he knew.

"I'm sure you'll be back in shape and out of here in a few months," said Jim. "It doesn't sound like you're too bad off."

"I guess you're right. I hope they take this cast off soon. I have had it on for almost two weeks now, and well, maybe it's just me, but something doesn't feel right down there." Bill pointed to his ankle.

"Doc Berg will probably change it tomorrow," said Childres.

COMING TO TERMS

It was happy hour at the club and the "Snake Pit" had their usual table. Everyone knew them, or of them, so doctors and nurses were constantly stopping by and asking them how things were going, or asking them to verify the latest rumor concerning The Pit. There was usually a little truth to everything, but by the time the stories filtered up to the other floors they were usually greatly exaggerated. However, nothing was ever denied regardless of how distorted the incident had become.

"Where are the girls?" It was Doc Berg. "I think this is the first time I've seen you guys alone."

"It's a little early yet," said Tom. "They'll be here in a little while."

"Good, that gives me a chance to talk to you alone. I'm glad you didn't bring Bill up here tonight.. We changed his cast today and his foot looks bad. The doctor who put the cast on in Vietnam wrapped it too tight in the wounded area, and his foot is badly infected. I'm giving him the strongest antibiotic we have, hoping it will clear up. You guys really need to go to work on him and keep his mind off his foot. I'm not sure just how strong he is so he is going to need help."

"We all know he is pretty worried about losing his foot," said Childres. "What do you think? Is there a chance it might have to come off?"

"It's possible, actually it's too early to tell yet. Like I said, we are giving him this antibiotic hoping it will clear up."

"Hey Childres, it's your turn to buy a round," said John. "I'm dying of thirst."

"Same thing, Doc?" Childres asked as he motioned for the waitress. Doc Berg gave him the affirmative sign.

John went over to the jukebox and began punching the buttons.

"Anyone want to make a bet on what song we're going to hear for the next half hour?" asked Jim.

"Yah, the Ballad of the Green Berets and the A Detachment," answered Tom.

Barry Saddler's "Green Berets" filled the club.

"It's going to be a long evening," said Doc Berg, grinning.

After both songs had played twice and the Green Berets was starting again, a tall lanky male nurse lieutenant went over to the jukebox and pulled the plug out of the wall.

"Hey you, come on over here," John yelled at him.

The Lieutenant ignored John, and went back to his table and rejoined five others sitting there. One of the female nurses with him patted him on the back, congratulating him on his brave deed.

"You know, I don't think he heard me," said John, getting up.

"Take it easy, John," said Childres. "Don't do anything that you might regret later."

"Don't worry, I've never regretted a thing in my life."

John walked over to the table and introduced himself.

"You know, I put eight quarters in that machine over there and all my songs have not played yet. If you didn't like my songs, you could at least have let me know. It was extremely rude of you to pull the plug. Now please go on over and plug it back in."

The Lieutenant was sizing John up. He was taller than John, but John outweighed him by at least fifty pounds.

"Look, we're tired of you war heroes coming up here taking over our club. That goddamn song stinks and we're sick of listening to it. " The others at the table agreed with him and gave him encouragement.

"I'm going to ask you once more to plug the machine back in," said John in a calm voice.

"Plug it in yourself," said the Lieutenant, turning away from John, and started talking to the others at the table, ignoring him. What happened next was a little confusing. But the first thing anyone heard was a loud gravely yell emanating from John's throat, as he picked the Lieutenant up, held him over his head and threw him up against the wall. The other two males sitting at the table rushed John, but he was waiting for them, and knocked both of them to the floor. The girls at the table were screaming.

"Hold it, John." It was Childres moving towards him. "That's enough."

"I only asked the good Lieutenant to plug in the jukebox. I guess he didn't hear me."

Doc Berg joined Childres at John's side. "Okay, let's sit down and relax. It's over with, folks, just a little misunderstanding." Doc Berg was trying to calm the others in the club down.

The club manager came over. "I should notify the MPs," he said in a shaking voice.

"No, it's not necessary," said Doc Berg. "I'll handle this." He walked over to the Lieutenant, who was just getting up. "Are you all right" he asked him. The Lieutenant indicated he was.

"Well, if I were you, I'd plug in that jukebox before he gets mad at you."

The Lieutenant looked at Doc Berg and slowly walked over and plugged the jukebox back in. Barry Sadler's voice filled the air once more.

"Hey, what's going on in here?" The girls walked in and seated themselves at the table.

"What's happened, why is everyone on edge?" Kris asked Pete. He told her about the incident.

"John, you should know better than to pick on a nurse. He is really a sweet guy. I'm surprised at you." Kris was mocking John.

"Someone buy these broads a drink," said John, "Maybe it will shut them up. I'm trying to listen to my favorite song."

The club had settled down and the club manager had returned to his office. The Lieutenant had rejoined his group and had quietly departed with them.

"You folks know I really didn't mean to get rough with him, I did ask him nicely to plug it in. I'm a gentle person." John was starting to lay it on kind of thick, an indicator that he was starting to feel his drinks.

"John, we all know that you are a gentle person." Kris was playing the game. "But we also know that you did some wonderful civic action type work in Vietnam. Isn't it called civic action, Pete?"

He had indicated that it was.

"Well, John, your reputation is well known in the "Snake Pit" about your little escapades with the Australian SAS (Special Air Services), namely the "007" game." Kris was now getting a sarcastic tone in her voice. "You could have done that poor Lieutenant in for good. I happened to be standing in the doorway with the rest of the girls when you grabbed him. I saw the look on your face. You could, or would just as well have killed him as anything."

"Hey, what does she know about that stuff? Pete, you'd better keep your mouth shut." The tension around the table was mounting.

"Since you got married to this broad, you have gotten what is called pussy whipped. I suggest you keep your trap shut or you could get a lot of people compromised, not to mention killed."

"John, no one meant for this to go this far," said Childres. "But since it has, let me set a few facts straight. No one has said a thing except for you. You have a problem and that is that you talk in your sleep, and especially when you come out of surgery. First, it was Whealen here who came in and took care of you when you had your nightmares, and later on Kris came in. We all know that you didn't step on a booby trapped 81 mm mortar shell. You still scream at night. Doc Berg here knows about it. You are very explicit when you talk. We just haven't mentioned it to you, just like we don't mention the rest of us. Tom here, we all know that he wasn't hit while sitting on top of an Army Personnel Carrier (APC) eating his lunch. He talks too much also, especially when he is on Demerol, or has had too much to drink."

"What the hell is going on here? I came up for a friendly happy hour, and it's turning into the Last Supper."

"Keep your voice down, John, we can talk about this in an intelligent way and get it over with once and for all," said Childres.

"I really don't talk, do I?" asked Tom with a worried look on his face.

"About as much as John and Pete," answered Whealen.

"Oh Christ, I have been here over a year and I thought it was all behind me," said Tom.

"You know, you will get your jump wings and the jump pay when your official files are formally declassified," said Doc Berg.

"I'm not going to belabor this, but we all know that you lost your leg when you jumped in to search for the records and codes in that plane that went down in the fall of '64 with 25 paratroopers aboard on the border of North Vietnam," said Whealen. "You were working for the Agency at the time, and the best we have been able to piece together is that you had had no jump training at all. That first jump was your last jump. The only thing that saved your life was the Special Forces reaction team, which went in to bail you out. Your partner was not so lucky, he was captured or killed. Correct me if I'm wrong."

"Jesus Christ," said Tom in utter disbelief. Pat was sitting next to him. She had tears in her eyes and had covered his hand with hers.

"Tom," she said, "It had to come out sooner or later. I'm glad it's out in the open."

"As for you, John Snyder, I'm sick and tired of hearing your rambling at night. Yes, it's no secret that we sleep together, or should I say used to sleep together." Whealen was getting worked up. "Where do you want me to start? I know the whole story about your boss Captain Krasnoff of the Australian SAS. How you went to your special school outside Nha Trang to learn how to kill without making any noise. Listen, I could write a book."

"Shut up, Marie, or I'll…."

"You'll what, John, take care of me? You know, that's the first time you have called me Marie in front of anyone in over a year. It used to be Whealen this, Whealen that. Oh, I'm sorry, you were always respectful of my rank. You also used to say Captain Whealen. Let me tell you, you lost your leg and when you thought you killed a Viet Cong leader and his body guards you got sloppy and the bodyguard waited for a chance and shot you."

John sat in silence not saying anything. He was staring at his bourbon and water. No one spoke for a while.

Childres broke the silence. "It's hard to sit here during a Happy Hour, safe and in peace, and realize that less than a twenty hour flight from here, Americans are dying and fighting the worst kind of war we have ever committed ourselves to, and wasting thousands of lives. I think history will record when this is all over that this will be our costliest and dirtiest war we have ever been engaged in. The French took four years to realize that they couldn't win. Not because their soldiers didn't fight well, but because their politicians wouldn't support them. And maybe rightfully so. But they bled dearly for their unpopular national policy. I think Pete here might have come closest to saying or predicting what might eventually happen in the States. Do you mind if I tell the story, Pete?"

Pete waved him on, indicating that it was all right.

"Well, Pete met an old Italian businessman in a small town in the Highlands of Vietnam, when he first arrived in country. Pete and his "A" detachment had contracted with the Italian for some construction work. To make a long story short, one day the Italian came out to the construction site and brought some beer with him. He and Pete were sipping a bottle when the Italian got serious and told Pete, "You American Special Forces are so proud and confident that you will win this war, and that you have all the answers. But let me tell you, I've been here for almost fifty years and these people that you are fighting are not in a hurry. If it takes them one year or twenty they will continue to fight. I admit they are not popular here in the Highlands amongst the Montagnards, but you Americans make so many mistakes.

"You kill President Diem. Yes, you killed him or had him

killed. The Vietnamese know this. But you see, no matter how bad Diem was in the eyes of the Americans, he was the only uniting or rallying point the Vietnamese had. You played right into the hands of the VC and the North Vietnamese. Ninety percent of the Vietnamese knew or had heard of Diem, and believe it or not, in their own strange Asiatic mind, loved and respected him, in spite of his many shortcomings. Who do they have now? We have had three coups in four months.

"The peasant out in the countryside doesn't have a radio or TV to find out who their leader is at the moment. The VC are amongst them spreading dissent and uncertainty. All the peasant wants is to be left alone and to grow his crops and raise his family. So if the VC promises him peace, or threatens him, he will go along with him, for the VC know that they must win the countryside first, the towns and cities will come later.

"As I said before, if it takes one year or twenty, the VC will prevail. But will you Americans? Can you afford to get bogged down 15,000 miles from home? Will the politicians support it? How about your people?

"I was in France in 1953, on vacation, when some of the French wounded soldiers were coming home from Vietnam. They were being off loaded from the trains in Paris. Do you know the attitude of the French people had gone completely against her Army? Encouraged no doubt by some of the politicians. They spat upon the wounded as they were being unloaded from the trains. So I say this to you, be careful, my proud American Green Beret, don't wear your heart on your sleeve. You could be spat upon by your people in not too many years. I hope not, but I feel you are in for a fight of much larger proportions than you realize today. Sure, these Mountain people love you. They are hated by the Vietnamese, yet they are the best fighters in Vietnam. They have more loyalty to you than to Saigon. So enjoy your popular war while it lasts, for I fear there are hard times ahead of you."

No one spoke for a few minutes.

"We've said a lot of words here tonight," said George, "much of it in anger. Most of the people here have been together for a year. We've had some good times, and some very bad times, pains that other people would not believe. You can't describe the pain of a bone transplant. We have loved and married the nurses. There had never been a secret in the "Snake Pit." We have all known about the screams at night or the ramblings when one of us came out of surgery, or talks in his sleep.

"But we have never confronted each other with those things. It's been a personal thing up to now. I always thought that when the day came for all of us to get out of here and go our separate ways, we would still keep in touch. But what I have seen here tonight leads me to believe that there will be no reunions or even Christmas cards. I don't know, maybe it's the attitude that's creeping across the nation. Maybe they have started spitting at us already. I do know that nothing will be the same in the "Snake Pit" after this evening, as much as we might try. I think the thing that kept us together was the trust and secrets we shared about each other.

"Don't get me wrong, I'm not blaming anyone here for breaking the bubble. Maybe it should have been broken a long time ago. We need to disperse, we have gotten so we think, or like to think that this is the real world. We feel secure and people come to look at us. We have the run of the hospital. Do you know what they tell the new student nurses that are enrolled in this new Army Nurse Program here? When you go down to the "Snake Pit" you will meet the real Vietnam heroes. Treat them special. If they want a back rub or TLC, give it to them, for they are what nursing is all about. Be friendly towards them. Am I lying, Doc? I had a young student 18 years old invite me to the motel so she could show me her true appreciation for what I had done for my country."

"You're right to a certain extent, George. They had gone a little overboard in their indoctrination of the students. But you have to realize that this is the first class and a lot of the instructors are caught up in the war, or patriotism, or whatever you want to call it."

"I don't care, Doc. It's not right. Don't get me wrong. I like a little TLC. I just don't want it thrown at me by some brainwashed kid, who doesn't know what's happening."

"Well, my glass is empty," said Perez, "After this sobering lecture, I feel like really tying one on. And George, don't be surprised if I throw myself at you tonight, and you'd better reciprocate, for believe me, I know what I'm doing and I'm not brainwashed. This is going to be one of those nights, kiddo."

Everyone laughed and ordered refills, and started talking at once. John got up and went over to the jukebox and played the "Ballad of the Green Berets." Everyone yelled and shook their fists at him.

Doc Berg leaned over to Kris and whispered, "I think the serious business for this evening is over with."

George's prediction that The Pit would never be the same came about slowly, but just the same, it was happening. The changes were subtle, and most of the "Snake Pit" members were indifferent. Brandon's assignment to the group was perhaps the most dramatic change. He had just arrived from the same war, but a definitely changed war. He related stories of Brigade size US Army units executing sweeps and search and destroy missions. Thousands of helicopters were now in Vietnam airlifting whole battalions, and even larger units. Brandon was part of the new war, and the others in the "Snake Pit" were part of the old war. A new era had emerged in Vietnam. It was now the US Army's war; it was no longer the war of the US Advisory effort.

Another change was the imminent departure of the "Snake

Pit" members. Childres and George were leaving within a week, as were John and Tom. Pete was leaving within a month.

Kris, now a Captain, had orders for Vietnam, and would depart in 90 days. She was staying until Pete was discharged. Then the two of them would be going on leave prior to her departure. Pete would be going to a six month school and would then join her in Vietnam.

Jim would be the only original member left, and it wouldn't be long before he would be leaving also. Jim and Tom were the only ones getting out of the Army; Tom going into business with his father, and Jim going to law school at the University of Tennessee. He and Linda were getting married in Memphis when he was discharged.

John had received a Branch transfer to AG. George and Childres had orders for Advanced School. Everyone was busy making plans and taking care of their futures. The "Snake Pit" was quiet.

No one was paying much attention to Brandon. His leg was still a touch and go situation. A Branch representative, a Lieutenant Colonel, had visited and briefed him on his career status.

"What's the good word, Brandon?" John asked.

"Well, I don't rightly understand it." It was obvious to everyone that Brandon was shook. "This Lieutenant Colonel informed me that I probably wouldn't be able to stay in the Infantry if they freeze my ankle. But that I probably could stay if they amputated and gave me a prosthesis. Does that make sense to you all?"

"Come on, are you sure you understood him correctly?" asked Childres.

"Why yes, I asked him three times. I'm going to have to talk with Doc Berg about this. I don't know, taking off my foot just don't sit right with me . I don't think I could ever transfer to another Branch."

"Oh shit, something is wrong here," said John. "Why don't you call Infantry Branch and see what they say. Get another recommendation."

"I think I will."

A week had elapsed and they decided to have a get together at the club, since this would be the last day they would all be together.

"The only one missing is nasty old Sandusky," said Tom.

"Yeah, can you imagine him flying for the Agency in Laos? That guy is a walking security risk. I'll bet he loves it. With the money he's hauling down, he can get a different tail every night," said John. "The last time he stopped by he was pretty excited about the job. He got the regular year leave from the Army, good money, and like he said, all he could steal."

"Why didn't Brandon come up? Is he okay, Doc?" asked John.

"Well, we're going to amputate his foot day after tomorrow. It's the best course in the long run. It would be very easy for him to develop another infection even after we freeze the ankle. He's pretty shook up about it," said Doc Berg. "But the final decision was his. He's a big boy now."

"Well, you heard what Infantry Branch told him, didn't you?" Childres cut in.

"Yes, he told me. In a way he's going to be more mobile with an artificial limb or foot, than if we froze his ankle. He's a slight person, and won't exert as much pressure as say John here, on his stump. So he will probably be better off. Those of you who will be around for a while longer better keep a close eye on him and keep his mind off his problems."

"He's not the strongest person, mentally, that is," said John. "He's pretty insecure."

"Well, let's change the subject and get another round," said

Tom. "This is supposed to be a happy occasion, getting out of here and back to normal life."

"I'll drink to that," said John.

They had stayed late at the club, but it was not the usual happy celebration associated with the "Snake Pit" members.

The next couple of weeks, Pete was busy with his clearance and making preparations for his and Kris' departure. His hand had gotten surprisingly strong and he was in better shape than he thought possible. The skin graft on his hand gave it an awkward appearance when he didn't have his shirt on, but otherwise no one could have guessed that there was anything unusual about it. Jim and he were now the only ones left of the old group. They had not moved anyone else into the area. Most of the time, Brandon was the only occupant, since Pete now spent most of his nights at the apartment and Jim stayed with Linda.

Brandon was not bearing up too well after the amputation. Bjorkvik had told Pete that if there were no dramatic change in his depression he would be moved up to the Psychiatric ward.

Pete made a stop at the Ward early in the morning he and Bjorkvik were to depart. When he checked in at the nurses' station there was nobody there. He proceeded down to the "Snake Pit." It was empty, but he heard a commotion coming from the bath/shower area. Walking slowly over to the door, he heard talking and orders being given. A medic rushed past him and out the "Snake Pit" door. He stuck his head in the shower room and saw Dr. Berg working on someone on the floor. There were several medics and the new nurse. Dr. Berg looked up and shook his head and got up slowly from the floor. He noticed Pete in the doorway and their eyes met. Pete heard voices behind him. Dr. Grange and another Dr. pushed by Pete and went over to Dr. Berg. They moved away from the others and talked. After a while Dr. Berg came over and informed the nurse to call the CID (Criminal Investigation Division) and have a representative come over immediately. Dr. Berg took Pete by the shoulder and steered him into the "Snake Pit."

"Brandon hung himself sometime early this morning. The best I can determine, it was about 4 hours ago."

Pete looked at Dr. Berg. "I guess Jim and I should have stayed closer to him and spent the nights here?"

"No, don't go there, Pete, this has nothing to do with you and Jim. All of you did your job trying to turn him around. Mrs. Foster found him hanging in the shower stall when she couldn't find him in the bed at her rounds. She is in shock. You may want to stop by and see her. I gave her a mild sedative and she is resting in the room next to the Nurses' Station."

Pete left not saying a word and headed for Mrs. Foster's room. He gently opened the door. Mrs. Foster was lying on the bed with a light blanket over her. Her eyes were open, but she seemed not to notice Pete coming to her bedside. He gently touched her and she took his hand and squeezed it.

"Can you answer a few questions? I have some forms I have to fill out before I can admit you to the "Snake Pit," said Pete with a twinkle in his eyes. "But since it's you, you already are a member so I guess they are not necessary."

"Oh Captain Compton," she grabbed him and pulled him down to her and held him for a few minutes. "I'm so glad it's you that came in. You always were my favorite. I don't want to talk about what happened in there. Please don't tell Kris until you are on vacation. She deserves to be off somewhere with you. You make the decision if and when you tell her. She is like me. We get too close to patients and it hurts too much."

"Ok, you win as always Mrs. Foster, but I do want to tell you one thing."

"What's that?" she looked confused.

"All of us in the 'Snake Pit" were afraid of you. That's why we always behaved cause you used to say you had an oak paddle in the office and you would use it if we misbehaved."

That got a smile on her face. "Lord, if I had used a paddle on you folks in The Pit each time you did something, why I don't think there are enough paddles in Washington, D.C., to have kept you in line."

Pete could tell she was in a better frame of mind. "Well, I'll tell you, Mrs. Foster, we were afraid of that paddle especially when Mrs. Blake covered for you on your vacation." That got a chuckle out of her.

"Lord, Cpt Compton, I miss you boys already and after what happened this morning nothing will be the same." Tears were in her eyes and Pete gave her Kleenex from the night stand.

"I think you missed your calling, Cpt Compton. You should have been a Dr., a psychologist. You have a way with people."

"Please don't tell Kris that. She thinks anyone who does what I do has lost his senses, and I want her to keep thinking that cause that way I can get away with just about anything."

"You can't fool me Cpt Compton. Kris is the luckiest girl in the world and you tell her that from me when you are out of here and on your vacation. She and I have had many a conversations about you."

"Oh!" Just then Dr. Berg walked in. "Everything alright? How are you feeling Mrs. Foster?" said Dr. Berg.

"Oh, I'm okay. It was such a shock when I walked in there, that poor boy," said Mrs. Foster.

"There are some people who will want to talk to you if you are up to it?" said Dr. Berg.

"Oh, I'm fine. Get this Captain out of here and get him on his way." Pete bent down and gave Mrs. Foster a kiss on the cheek. He walked out and touched Dr. Berg's shoulder and left.

EPILOGUE

"Major Compton! Major Compton!" It was the woman behind the admittance desk. "You must have been daydreaming," she said as he walked up to the desk. "I've been trying to get your attention for quite a while. I'm sorry it took so long to confirm your bed, but we're really filled up around here these days. What with the way things are going on in Vietnam and all."

He took the forms offered him, thanked her and walked away toward the stairs at the end of the hallway.

"Do you know the way to get down there," she yelled after him.

He didn't bother answering her; he just waived the admittance forms over his head. Christ, did he ever know how to get to the "Snake Pit." As he walked down the corridor, he recognized one of the Red Cross girls. She had taken care of the "Snake Pit." He was tempted to say something to her, but changed his mind.

He pushed open the doors to Ward #1. It all looked the

same. Walking into the nurses' station, he stopped cold. Mrs. Foster was standing directly in front of him.

"My Lord, it can't be. My Lord, it is! Captain Compton, is it really you?" She threw her arms around him. He kissed her cheek, holding her ample body close to him.

"How long has it been? It must be over 3 years," she said, pushing him away, still holding his hands.

He told her it was a long time.

"Here, give me those forms, and I'll take you down to the "Snake Pit". I have a million questions to ask you."

She led him down to the area and introduced him to the occupants. There were nine beds now, all occupied but one.

"George's old bed is vacant, how is that for a memory?"

He put his things away, while she explained to the others that he was one of the original members of the "Snake Pit," and had been part of the original group that named it - which everyone in the hospital was still talking about. Mrs. Foster closed the curtains around the bed.

"Is it still Captain?" she asked.

He told her it was now Major.

"I can't keep up with all these ranks. What I wanted to tell you was how sorry I am about Kris. We all heard about it here. I loved that girl like my own. She was the best nurse we ever had on this ward. I know I don't have to tell you that. I just can't figure out why she had to be the one. Oh Lord, sometimes I just don't understand." Tears were streaming down her cheeks as she talked.

"Look at me, I'm such a silly goose, but I still think about you and her, in fact, all of you. This place has never been the same, like it was when you were here before. These new patients, all they do is complain. They're a different breed, Major Compton. They're not real soldiers." She was laughing with tears still streaming down her face. "There hasn't been a girl in these beds since you boys left."

Mrs. Foster pulled back the curtains part way. "I have to go now. I left some forms on the nightstand. You have to take them up to the lab in the morning, but you know all that." Mrs. Foster walked out of the "Snake Pit."

He changed into pajamas, and lay down on the bed. He could tell that the others were watching him. He just didn't feel like talking. Mrs. Foster had reopened a deep wound that he thought he had partially gotten over. How ironic to be back in the same room.

Kris' death had been very painful for him. She had been in Vietnam three months when he had arrived. She had been in route to the Air Force Base to meet him when the chopper she had been flying in had crashed. The official report had read, no survivors, cause unknown. Hostile action probable. He had taken her back and buried her in Minnesota, and had returned to Vietnam immediately. The Army had told him he did not have to go back, but he insisted.

It was hard to believe that all of it had happened to him. His year in Vietnam had been a bitter one for him. He had volunteered for all the missions that had come up. Finally, he was starting to get a reputation as a vengeance seeker and when he had three months to go had been transferred to Saigon to a safer environment. His old wounds had started giving him problems, and so here he was back in the old "Snake Pit."

He must have dozed off, for he felt someone's hand on his shoulder and a voice asking him if he would like to have some dinner.

He opened his eyes slowly. Standing next to his bed was a young nurse smiling down at him. "You have been here before, Major Compton, haven't you? I hope your stay this time will be a little more pleasant for you." He was startled at the resemblance to Kris. His mind was racing. Shutting his eyes for a second, thinking he was dreaming, but when he opened them she was still there.

She was fairly tall with light red hair and a pretty face. "I remember you from before. I was a student nurse when you were here then. As a matter of fact, I used to give you back rubs. But you couldn't possibly remember that."

He told her he would like some dinner, and yes, he did recall the times she had given him back rubs. She seemed pleased and departed to get his dinner. He closed his eyes. It was not going to happen again. It was not going to happen to him again. This time he was going to be a patient, and get out of there, and that was all.

CPSIA information can be obtained
at www.ICGtesting.com
Printed in the USA
LVHW082321300819
629552LV00001B/3/P

9 781733 314916